THE BLACK BOX

A Novel

Cliff Jackman

Manor House

Library and Archives Canada Cataloguing in Publication

Jackman, Cliff, 1980-
          The black box : a novel / Cliff Jackman.

ISBN 978-1-897453-23-0

          I. Title.

PS8619.A224B53 2012   C813'.6   C2012-907726-7

Published November 15, 2012: Manor House Publishing Inc.,
452 Cottingham Crescent, Ancaster, ON, CANADA, L9G 3V6
905-648-2193 wwww.manor-house.biz

Cover Design: Donovan Davie based on original art created
by Donovan Davie

We acknowledge the financial support of the Government of
Canada through the Canada Book Fund (CBF) for our
publishing activities.

This is a work of fiction – no connection or similarity with
anyone alive or deceased is intended or implied.

Until recently Enron's attitude, expressed with barely concealed disdain, was that anyone who couldn't understand its business just didn't "get it." "Our business is not a black box," Jeff Skilling told me. "It's very simple to model." And at the time, many Wall Street analysts who followed the company were content to go along. Now that it's clear that the company wasn't what it appeared, the new cliché is that Enron's business was incredibly complicated - perhaps even too complicated for its founder Ken Lay to understand. Which leads to a basic question: why were so many people willing to believe in something that so few actually understood?

Bethany McLean

Au fond, tout les films noirs ont la même signification: il n'y a rien de plus solitaire dans ce monde que d'avoir une mauvaise conscience.

Jean-Pierre Melville

Dedication

On August 25, 2011, Bruce Goldstein was found dead in David A. Balfour Park beneath Glen Road Bridge, his broken body crumpled up like a piece of paper someone tried to throw in a garbage can, but missed. Brucie had been just short of his eighteenth birthday, and by all accounts he'd been a well-liked, happy kid. The fall had killed him but his father didn't believe it was a suicide and so he asked me and Dean to look into it. This is the story of what we found.

I decided to write this book for a few reasons. Money, first of all, I guess. Who doesn't like money? It's also a chance to set the record straight, since a lot of that media coverage was total bullshit. And although you might not know it by looking at me, or by talking with me, or even by hanging out with me for years, I have always been something of a writer. I kept a journal my whole life and it's pretty bitching to get to publish a book.

But the more I stare at this screen, the more I think that the real reason I'm writing this book is to get something out of me. Like, if I tell this story, I might be able to make sense of some of the things that people did, including me, that I can hardly believe. Dean says what everyone really wants is to be understood. Of course, he also says no one understands anyone else, the gloomy bastard.

A few years back, believe it or not, Dean and I investigated a different mysterious death back in California. I'm not going to get into that here, but let's just say it didn't end well and I thought Dean had been hurt so bad he would never recover. I was wrong. When I saw Dean again in September 2011, he seemed like he'd come all the way back. But now, after Brucie, things are tough for him again.

I think he'll get better. I'm just not really sure that's for the best. Maybe it would be better if our broken hearts never did mend. Otherwise, we're like that guy who pissed off Zeus, getting our guts ripped out, having them grow back, and getting them ripped out all over again the next day. Dean doesn't know how to live. He only knows one way to roll, in his heart, and it's a bruising way to go. This book won't make things easier for him, but it's in his honour. I feel for you buddy. Hang in there.

1

It's tough to know exactly how to start. I'm not in favour of just giving everyone's life history. So here's my thinking: I never would have got hired to investigate Brucie's death if I hadn't bumped into Dean at the Duke of Devon.

And I never would have been at the Duke of Devon if Mikey Gottlieb hadn't taken me out for drinks.

And Mikey wouldn't have taken me out if I hadn't busted Martin Cole on the Slip 'n Slide. So I'll start with that.

Picture me wearing a cheap tan suit with a rumpled blue shirt and a tie with a monkey on it. I'm black, I've got a shaved head, and (let's not kid ourselves here) I'm pretty fucking fat. I'm sitting behind the wheel of my Hyundai Accent on a rural road in Oro-Medonte. The packaging from a combo meal at Harvey's is in the backseat, next to my crumpled copy of *Half-Blood Blues*. I'm bored, and I'm already kind of hungry again. Mostly I'm playing Angry Birds on my iPhone, but every now and then I lift my head to watch the house.

It was a little raised bungalow made of pink brick. The grass on the front yard was long, approaching hay field territory. An elderly deck, made of cedar so neglected that it had turned a rotten shade of grey, jutted out from the side and an old car was parked on the lawn. Through the windows I could see that the interior was crowded with stuff.

I spent a lot of time in houses like that growing up. The piles of magazines, old sports equipment, Tupperware. Being poor in America (or Canada, I guess) doesn't mean you don't have lots of stuff. Instead, it's like you can't get rid of anything; like you're drowning in junk.

The lawyers I work for don't have a lot of sympathy for people like the Cole family. They talk about how their behavior drives up everyone's premiums, and so on. And I suppose there's not much you can really say about that. Still, I can't help but sympathize. When you're choking on a wave of crap like that, you do whatever you've got to do to get from out under.

The sliding screen door that opened onto the deck banged open and the family barged out. I waited in my car, half-hidden from their view by the big weeping willow on the edge of their property, until I saw Martin was out with them. The big guy was skipping as nimbly as a ballerina. I got out, bringing my camera with me, and moved over to the fence line as stealthily as I could.

Martin Cole was fatter than me, with orange hair that was fading into grey. Thick glasses were perched on his nose and he gave off the proud, aggressive air of a little fighting dog. He was moving without the pain and difficulty that had characterized his appearances in court, and shouting and waving his hands at his numerous chubby children.

As best as I was able, I hid my fat ass behind an old fence post. Then I took out my camera and started recording video, while taking still pictures at the same time.

All of the Cole clan was dressed in swimsuits, which I thought was odd, since they didn't have a pool, and the nearest body of water was Lake Simcoe, a good drive away. But then the two eldest Cole daughters came out carrying a rolled-up yellow plastic sheet, and I started to giggle.

Martin, you fucking idiot, I thought.

They unfolded the Slip 'n Slide so that it ran down towards me. One daughter sprayed it with water from the hose until it got nice and slick, and the kids started hurling themselves at it so crazily that I kind of worried that one of them would suffer a spinal injury for real.

Martin was last. His kids were dancing around him, giggling and shrieking and shoving him with their wet hands, while Ron ran back and forth dodging them. Finally he sprinted towards the strip of yellow plastic, flopped down face first, and shot towards me like a bullet. My finger was clicking on the button like mad, and if you look at the photos in sequence, you can see his expression change, from happiness to surprise to shock and to anger, as he saw me watching him.

I'll give the fat bastard credit. He was pretty quick to bounce up to his feet, especially for someone who allegedly had such a nasty case of fibromyalgia and whiplash. And then he ran towards me, roaring like a bull, his orange mullet bouncing on the back of his neck, and his red fat body glistening like a sea lion that had flopped out of the ocean onto a rock. Behind him followed the screaming horde. It was like I'd disturbed some redneck version of the Wild Hunt.

So I started backing up towards my car, but I kept the camera on old Martin. How could I not? I'd come here to film him behaving in a way which was inconsistent with his claims about his injury, and this certainly fit the bill.

"Get off my fucking property, you nigger!"" he shouted.

"Hey!" I said. "Watch your mouth."

"Get off my property!"

"I'm not on your property," I said. "I'm on the road!"

Now he was right up in my face, filling my little viewfinder.

"Gimme that camera," Martin said.

"Fuck off!" I said.

"I said give it to me!" Martin shouted, and lunged. I pushed at him, and turned away, sheltering the camera with my body, but he was a powerful, almost athletic dude, and I'm not sure I could have taken him even on my own. When all of the kids arrived, boys and girls, and started kicking and punching and slapping me, it wasn't much of a contest. Ron yanked the camera away, threw it down on the ground, and stomped on it with one bare (but exceedingly calloused) foot.

"Hey motherfucker," I said. "You're going to have to pay for that."

But then I saw Martin's wife running over. She was a big old girl, and she was jiggling every which way with the effort. Above her head she was carrying a shotgun like a Zulu matron with her husband's spear.

"Oh shit," I said, and shoved everyone away with a burst of panicky strength and got back in my car. The kids were smacking the windows with their hands when I turned the key in the ignition and jumped on the gas. I took one glance over my shoulder to make sure I'd hadn't run any of them over and then I gunned it as hard as you can gun a Hyundai.

Thankfully, they didn't shoot at me.

I only drove for about five minutes before I had to pull over. The suspense was killing me. I brought up my laptop from the back seat and checked the folder that I kept my videos in. Modern technology is certainly amazing. Everything was safely in the cloud.

When I saw the picture of Martin staring at me in dismay from the Slip 'n Slide, I started to laugh. The video was even funnier, and I laughed harder. Not a bad morning's work, really. I was still giggling when I drove down the 400, slick with well water and hillbilly sweat. I pretty much laughed all the way back to the city.

2

Mikey looked up when I came in his office. He was a good looking kid, mixed race, with a Jewish dad and a black mom. His skin was light brown and he had a big afro (or jew-fro, I guess). The cuffs of his blue, tailored shirt were rolled up, displaying his Seiko watch, and he wasn't wearing a tie. His office was as bereft of decorations as a prison cell, but the view from 18 floors up wasn't anything to sneeze at, not for a country boy like me anyway.

"Terrell," he said, "I'm right in the middle of something."

"Oh bullshit," I said. Junior lawyers were always right in the middle of something. I closed the door behind me, pushed some boxes off the spare chair onto the floor, sat down and opened my computer. "You seriously have to see this."

"Terrell," Mikey groaned in his Eeyore voice. "I'm getting totally slammed here. I'm going to be here all weekend."

"Just check this out," I said. "God. It's only going to take five minutes." I booted up the video.
Mikey sighed, and asked: "What file is this for?"

"Cole," I replied.

The look on Mikey's face slowly changed from one of deep mourning to one of bemusement.
"A Slip 'n Slide?" he asked, looking at me with the wide eyes of a kid who just got a Nintendo for Christmas.

"Just wait," I said, giggling. On the corner of his desk there was a plastic jar bearing the Blue Jays logo that contained a pint of sunflower seeds. I helped myself.
We got to the part where Martin Cole charged me. Now Mikey had thrown his head back and his eyes were as wide as they

could get. I started laughing uproariously and spitting seeds and shell all over the ground.

"Oh my goodness," Mikey said. "He used the n-word."

"I know, right? What a bastard."

"You have got to be kidding me!" Mikey said, grabbing his fro with both hands.

"Check out some of the still shots."

We worked through the pictures of Martin on the slide, till we got to the one where he was looking at me in shock.

"I want to make that my desktop wallpaper," Mikey said.

"So there you go," I said. "You got anything to drink here? Do you still have that scotch?"

Mikey looked at me for a moment, and said: "Well, fine. Let's go get a drink."

"I thought you had work."

"Oh, fuck it," Mikey said. "I'll be in all day tomorrow anyway. Everyone's down at the Duke."

"Which one?" I asked.

"The Duke of Devon," he replied. "Let's go now so we can get a seat on the patio."

It was 4:30 on a Thursday in mid-September, and the sky was blue as a baby's eye, so we definitely had to get moving if we wanted to sit outside.

A very pretty dark-haired girl, big chested, smiled at us as we came out of Mikey's office.

"What were you two laughing about?" she asked.

"Come to the Duke," I said. "We'll tell you all about it!"

Once we were in the elevator, I asked:

"Who was that chick?"

"Desiree," Mikey said, and shook his head and rolled his eyes comically. "She's killing me!"

"Is she a student?"

"Yes," Mikey said, and then added in a dejected tone: "She's engaged."

"Well so what?"

"Oh no," Mikey said, "not with this princess. Her wedding is going to cost $100,000. She is in my office talking about photographers every day. You need some serious dinero to get with that girl."

"Hey man," I said. "Anything's possible."

We came out into the sunshine and started heading south-east. Even though I come down there a lot, I always feel a little weird in the financial district. The buildings are so tall you feel like you're at the bottom of canyon, or maybe even under the sea. Unless it's noon it can be tough for the sunlight to get through, so you can be cold in the middle of the day.

We walked through the TD Centre, three tall black metal buildings built around a courtyard. Since it was the southernmost of the main office buildings, the patio we were going to (on its south side) caught the most sun.

"How are your investments going?" I asked. "Maybe you'll be able to afford to steal this chick away."

"Don't ask," Mikey said. "I thought I was going to get my money out of Edenfree. But the OSC just cease-traded it again, so I'm fucked, basically."

"Well, you can always go back to poker," I said.

"Yeah," Mikey said. "I might as well."

The Duke of Devon was mostly underground, in the system of underground hallways and stores that connected all the big buildings in downtown Toronto, but its patio poked above ground like the observation deck of a submarine. I didn't much care for the bar, with its nine dollar pints of London Pride, huffy waitresses in tartan skirts, and douchey suit-wearing clientele. But you can't get lawyers to walk more than thirty seconds from their offices, and anyway, it was a nice day to drink outside. We told the hostess we were meeting some friends, waved to Mikey's buddies, and made our way to the bar.

"I got this one, Delacroix," Mikey said and motioned to the bartender. "Two boilermakers, please."

"Aw nasty," I said.

I think it was like 36 bucks. Mikey paid, and we pounded our shots of JD, clinked our bottles of Bud, and turned around to find our seats.

And then I saw Dean.

3

I hadn't seen Dean for eight years, not so much as a picture on Facebook. He looked older. A lot of grey was mixed into his dark hair, which was shorter than I remembered. His face was lean and there were deep lines around his eyes. And his clothes! I'd never seen Dean in a suit before, but there he was, dressed to the nines, tie and all, never mind that it was Thursday and he was on the patio.

The other people at his table were very young, some of the youngest at the bar, and they were all dressed up too. A couple pitchers of beer sat between them but Dean was drinking a Bloody Mary.

One of the young guys Dean was sitting with, a husky kid with curly blond hair and beard, noticed me gawking and pointed me out. Dean turned around and looked at me. For a moment he didn't do anything and I felt this terrible disappointment. He's going to pretend he doesn't remember me, I thought.

But then his face changed, and he jerked in his seat and knocked his drink over. Tomato juice ran across the table and the kids all jumped out of their seats. Dean didn't move. He kept staring at me.

"Holy shit," I said.

"You know that guy?" Mikey said, at my elbow.

Dean stood up. He noticed the spill by now, and looked around for something to clean it with, but the waitress was already on her way, and so he headed over to me.

"Terrell?" he asked.

I still didn't know whether he was happy to see me.

"Dean?" I asked.

And then he grinned, and all the eight years fell of his face. "Dude," he said. "What the fuck?"

I started laughing and hugged him and lifted him off the ground. When I put him down he was still staring at me, with that look of wonder.

"What are you doing here?" he asked.
"I live here!" I said. "I'm a private detective."
"What?" he said. "No way!"
"What about you?" I asked.
"I'm an articling student," he said.
"What?"
"Yeah. I went to law school down in California. I wrote the bar and practiced for a couple of years. Then I wanted to make a move. I know a lawyer up here at a pretty good firm, so they're taking me on."

"Which firm?"
"Stewart Brubaker Phillips."
"Wow! Congrats. That's the big time."

"I'm going to go sit down," Mikey said when it became clear an introduction was not forthcoming, and left.

I was so excited that I leaned forward and hugged Dean again. He laughed.
"Let's get a drink," I said. "Man I can't believe it's you."
We walked up to the bar.
"I'll have a virgin Caesar," Dean said.
"Virgin?" I cried. "Fuck that. No virgin anything for Dean today."
Dean smiled and reached into his pocket and took out his keys. He had a funny looking plastic key chain.
"Five years buddy," he said.

"Five years what?" I replied, stupidly, and then I said: "Oh! You're clean?"

"Yep."

"Not just the …"

"Not just that. Everything."

"Whoa. Isn't that a bit extreme?"

"Not as extreme as it was before," he said.

I couldn't disagree with that.

"The rule is I can have wine, but only at home," Dean said "And I never have three bottles in my house."

"Well, congrats buddy! I was really worried about you."

"Yeah well," he said, smiling, "I pulled through. With the help of a good woman."

"Who is this woman?"

"Someone you know."

"Really? Who?"

"Come over for dinner on Saturday," Dean said. "You can meet her."

"All right," I said.

"What's your number?" Dean asked.

I gave him both, my Blackberry and my iPhone.

"Two-phone Terrell?" Dean asked, smiling.

"I got the Blackberry through work right after I signed a three year contract," I complained.

The bartender set his drink down and Dean picked it up. For a moment I caught sight of one of his tattoos on his wrist, and then it was gone.

"Oh," Dean said. "I know I probably don't have to tell you this, so don't get offended or anything. But ix-nay on the Industry–hay."

"C'mon son," I said.

We clinked his glass to my bottle and made our way over to his table.

"Hey everybody," Dean said. "This is my friend Terrell from California."

All of the students smiled and waved.

"Hey!" I said.

"How do you know Dean?" one of the girls asked.

"We worked together," I said, and then thought: shit.

"Doing what?" she asked.

I hesitated, and then said: "Construction."

"I thought you worked in a bank," the blond guy asked, the one who had spotted me. Up close, he looked like an albino satyr; there was a twinkle of mischief in his eye.

"It was just a temporary thing," Dean said.

The satyr nodded.

"And now what do you do?" the girl asked.

"I'm a private detective," I said.

Everyone made appreciative noises. Being a private investigator sounds more glamorous than it is, unless the person you're talking to is in a union.

The topic changed to the Leafs' chances. Dean and I didn't say much, we couldn't talk in front of everyone, and after a few minutes he looked at his watch and smiled at me.

"Gotta run," he said. "I have to go help with the kids."

"Kids?" I exclaimed. "As in more than one?"

"See you Saturday," he said. "Look me up online and send me an e-mail."

"Hold on," I said, "I'll come with you."

Unfortunately, getting off the bench involved pulling my legs from under the table and with my belly I ran into a little difficulty.

Dean watched me with amusement.

"Dude," he said. "You got fat."

On the way to the exit we passed Mikey and his buddies. Mikey waved and a girl sitting at his table turned around to look at us. It was Desiree.

"Be right with you," I said. "I'm just saying goodbye to my buddy."

I turned to Dean to shake his hand but to my surprise he looked really upset. Shocked, like he'd seen a ghost. And then it struck me that Desiree looked a little like Tanya. Not like they were twins or anything, but similar. The hair mostly.

Dean noticed me looking at him and he tried to smile, but I could tell he was a little shaken up.

"Do you think of her often?" I asked.

"No, no," he said. "Just right after seeing you, you know."

"Right," I said.

We hugged and he left.

Then I sat down with Mikey and his buds. And we drank, a lot. It was one of those nights that just get away from you. We stayed on that patio until they were closing, at one in the morning, and then Mikey, visibly weaving on his feet and waving his hands like he was conducting an invisible orchestra, started trying to rally everyone over to the Brant House.

Now the Brant House sucks even harder than the Duke. It's one of those clubs where they charge a ten-dollar cover and won't let you in if you're wearing the wrong shoes, and then you get in, and you're like, this is it? This is a dark, noisy cave. But I was pretty drunk and I had my eye on a girl who'd joined us. Only girl was stretching it. She was older than me and a divorcee. Ridden hard and put away wet, you might say. But I've never been a picky man, not even back when I could afford to be. And this lady was funny, and cynical, and she had a big personality.

We sat across from one another and talked a long time. I had her laughing and everything. She even started touching my knee under the table. I was ready to close the deal right there, but she wanted to dance. To dance! So what was a brother to do?

At the Brant House, who should I run into but the blond satyr. I couldn't say I was surprised; he hadn't struck me as the type to go to bed early. His name was Matty. We shouted at each other over the driving bass.

"Any friend of Dean's is a friend of mine," he said.

"Likewise." I said.

"Can I ask you something?"

"What?"

"I'm worried you'll get offended."

"Is it racist?"

"No. Well, maybe."

"Hmm."

"It's not racist but it might be insensitive."

"I don't know dude."

"All right, I'm going to ask, but before you get mad, remember I'm from Newfoundland and I don't know any better."

I laughed.

"Have you ever been in a porno?"

I assumed an amused expression.

"No man," I said. "I can't act in porno. I can't get insured. My dick's too big."

He laughed hysterically, but fuck me, he was getting out his iPhone.

"But I saw this video," he said, "and the guy looks just like you."

So I crowded around to look, thankful it was just the two of us, and of course, there I was, considerably trimmer, pumping away, that focused, constipated look on my face. Fortunately, I was rarely on the screen. The camera mainly focused on the girl (Lily she'd called herself) as she assumed a variety of poses that were a lot less erotic to perform than they were to look at.

"He does look like you!" he said. "He does!"

"Well Matty," I said, "I guess we all look the same to a Newfie like you."

My date was off dancing. Every now and then she looked over at me and waved. After Matty wandered off to get us some shots, I waved back at her.

When she turned away I went outside and headed east on King, passed all the crowds lined up at the entrances to the clubs. When I hit University I turned north to Adelaide and went to Smokes. I ordered a large pulled pork poutine and ate it outside, watching the girls walk by in their shiny miniskirts, tottering on their high heels. Just another night out in the city.

4

Normally poutine really does the trick for me, hangover-wise, but when I woke up Friday morning, I felt like ten pounds of shit in a five pound bag. Fortunately, I had nothing to do but type up a report for the Cole thing. I spent the day in my office with the door closed, alternating between the report and my fantasy football team, until my boss barged in without knocking. His name was Alan King, and he was a tall, skinny ex-cop with a moustache who always reminded me of J. Jonah Jameson from Spider-man.

"Change of plans," Alan said.

"What plans?"

"Whatever your plans were five seconds ago," Alan said. "Here is your new plan. Go downtown and see Jay Goldstein."

"Who?" I asked.

"Jay Goldstein. Corporate lawyer with Stewart Brubaker Phillips. Very, very prominent corporate lawyer. Top ten in Canada. Called me and asked for you specifically. So you will go."

"What the fuck? It's Friday at 4 o'clock."

"I know, my beloved apprentice, but Stewarts is the richest and most expensive firm in the country, so if they had asked me for the tip of your dick, we'd be sending it down via same-day courier. You should be thankful they asked for you to come in person."

"What do they want with me?" I asked.

"Who knows? Like I said, Goldstein's not a litigator. Maybe it's personal? Who the hell cares? Just get down there."

"Come on, Alan," I said.

"No, you come on! You gotta admit this is a big one. You bring in SB fucking P as a client for this firm, you're a fucking rainmaker. It'll be King and Delacroix on the door!"

"Suck my dick," I said. Or words to that effect. Still, you couldn't say no to Alan. He took me on as an office boy before I was even a permanent resident. He was the boss.

Stewarts' lobby wasn't as nice as you'd expect for such a fancy, rich firm. Beige walls and bland abstract art. The receptionist was old with orange hair. She smiled at me as I came up, and then said that I should take a seat, someone would come up for me shortly.

I amused myself with the newspaper and with the view (Stewarts was on the 44th floor of First Canadian Place) until a woman came up the spiral staircase and brought me down to meet the great man himself.

Jay looked to be closing in on sixty. He was a husky guy, stooped at the shoulders, with an infectious, shy smile. You couldn't tell how smart he was by talking to him, and I mean that as a compliment. He never used a ten dollar word where a two dollar one would do.

The office was lined with knickknacks, crazy things. Lots of action figures of superheroes, including a big plastic Aquaman, and also pictures of his family. Looked like it was just him, his wife, and his boy. A picture of the three of them in the autumn sat prominently on his desk.

I shook his hand. His grip was gentle.

"Nice to meet you Mr. Delacroix," he said.

"Nice to meet you too, Mr. Goldstein," I said.

"How's your week been?"

"Pretty good," I said. "I'm working on an insurance case, personal injury. Yesterday I busted this guy who said he could barely walk. He was on a Slip 'n Slide."

I laughed, but Jay just smiled. I noticed how wan he looked, how tired.

"Well," Jay said, "you'll eventually see everything in this business."

There was a knock at the door and Dean came inside.

"Hey Jay," he began, and then he caught sight of me. The expression on his face was clear: what the fuck did you do?

"Come in, shut the door," Jay said. "You're not in trouble."

Dean did as he was asked.

"I heard about how Mr. Delacroix met the students last night," Jay said, "and I was about to hire a private detective anyway."

Now Dean looked unnaturally still. I knew that look. He had figured out what was going on. I still had no idea.

"Terrell," Jay said to me, "you should know that a couple of weeks ago my son died."

"Oh," I said. "I'm so sorry."

He lowered his head, accepting my sympathy, and went on.

"He fell off Glen Road Bridge, near our home, around Mount Pleasant and Bloor. The police investigated and the detective wanted to rule it suicide. I had a little trouble accepting that. I don't believe he could have been suicidal without me knowing about it."

He paused as if I would say something, but I didn't. So he went on.

"Anyway, the detective and I had a disagreement about it. It ended up staying a suspicious death. Just a few days ago I got some credit card bills, for my son. His mail is still coming, you know. So I opened them, I have to, I have to open all his mail now, and I saw that he'd run up 25 thousand dollars in credit card debt. And there were all these charges I didn't understand. And I'm tired of dealing with the police on this. I think they're tired of me too. So I'd like to hire you to look into it for me."

"Okay," I said. "Can I be honest? This is not what I normally do. You remember the Slip 'n Slide thing I just told you about?"

"Well," Jay said. "You'd be doing it with Dean. Just like you did back in California."

I looked at Dean and he looked back at me. I don't know what he was thinking. To be honest, I didn't even know what I was thinking. Other than: *this is fucked up*.

"Dean told me a bit about it when we hired him," Jay said.

"Okay Jay," Dean said. "How do I square it with work?"

"I'm going to set up a file here," Jay said. "Bill your time to that. I'll do the same thing with Terrell's fees."

"Is Arthur okay with that?" Dean said.

"I'll take care of Arthur," Jay said. "And I'll take care of you too. I don't want you to be worried about the time this takes."

Dean nodded.

"Want us to come over tomorrow maybe?" Dean said. "To check out where it happened, see his room? Get some of the details from you?"

"Sure," Jay said. "You know where I live."

"Okay," Dean said. "If it's what you want, Jay, we'll do it."

Jay nodded.

"Thank you. I know this wasn't a suicide. I think you'll see."

"There are some forms you have to sign," I started, but Dean gave me an annoyed look and waved his hand.

"We'll take care of all that," Jay said.

"Okay," Dean said. "See you tomorrow at one."

We stood up to go. Before we left, Jay said:

"What was the story again with the murder in California?"

Dean didn't say anything for a while. I sure as shit wasn't going to answer.

"It was in Nevada, actually," Dean said. "Near Vegas."

"And you never found out who did it?"

"No," Dean said. "We could never prove it."

"That's not what I asked you."

"Sure it is," Dean said. "If we couldn't prove it, then by definition, we didn't know."

Dean waited for the briefest moment for Jay to ask another question, and then brushed out of the room. I followed him.

After we were a few steps down the hall he looked back at me and smiled, that good old Dean smile, so genuine and kind, even though it looked like a quick wince of pain.

"Can you believe this shit?" he asked.

"I'm sorry Dean," I said.

"Ah, well, for what?" he said. "It'll be great. Just like old times."

I didn't say: that's what I'm afraid of.

5

Jay lived on a quiet street just a short jaunt from Bloor. The house was clearly pretty old, made of big gray stones, but it had been extensively renovated with long, angular windows and a skylight. The doorbell played a piece of classical music.

"Espresso?" Jay asked as he let us in.

We sat on leather couches in the solarium and looked out on the magnificent yard through a wall of clear glass. A couple of cardboard boxes sat on the coffee table along with a pile of letters that had been opened and then put back in their envelopes.

"So," Dean asked, "I can get the basic story from the cop, hopefully, when we call him up. But if you don't mind …"
"Not at all, "Jay said.

He ran through the story for us. Brucie had been very happy. He was going to go to school at Georgetown in the fall. Towards the end of August he got very upset. Wouldn't leave his room, wouldn't eat, wouldn't change his clothes, but wouldn't say why. The morning of August 26, Jay and his wife woke up and ate breakfast and then Jay left for work. His wife, Susan, went up to knock on Brucie's door and he wasn't there. She called his phone but no one answered. When she saw the commotion down the street, she realized what was going on.

"I wouldn't say the detective did a bad job," Jay said. "His name was Aston. Little guy, really muscular. He went up and down the block asking questions. No one had seen or heard anything. He went through Brucie's stuff, didn't see anything. No note. He talked to Susan and me. When the report came back from the autopsy that there was no sign of a struggle, he wanted to rule it a suicide. And it was only then that I really had a problem."

"Okay," Dean said.

"Now we're opening the mail that was comes in for Brucie. It looks like he has 25 thousand dollars in credit card debt. On four different cards."

"Wow," Dean said, as he browsed through the mail.

"There's a lot of charges on it I don't understand," Jay said. "Looks like they're to a Moneris machine licensed to an individual. I disputed the charges. Haven't heard back from anyone yet."

"Did you take these statements to the cop?" I asked.

"No," Jay said. "My relationship with Detective Aston was not good. He's stubborn, and I was very emotional. I thought I could do this on my own. But, ah, I think I realized I couldn't."

His voice was breaking a bit.

"Ah, also, you should know. My wife doesn't know I'm doing this. She's in Florida right now. It was very hard on her too. I guess, Terrell, you might not know, Brucie was our only child. It's kind of hard to deal with"

"Of course," I said

"So when I found this, I got very excited. I was talking to her about it. And she got very upset. She just wants this to be over. But I can't, I just can't."

I nodded.

"Anyway, that's where things are at." Jay said.

"What's in the boxes?" Dean asked.

"Some things Brucie had on him when he died. His phone, his wallet. They also found something very odd in his room. A bug. Not like an insect. An electronic tracking device. An old one."

"Really?" I said. I opened up the box and took it out. Yeah, there it was, about the size of a deck of playing cards. I'm kind of a nut for that sort of thing. I recognized it as an old Russian model.

"Weird," I said.

"Anything else?" Dean asked.

"Yeah, there was one last thing. Apparently a couple of days before Brucie died, he'd called up our cleaning lady. He was desperate, kept asking her about a black box."

"A black box?"

"Yes, where's the black box? He said it was under his bed but now it was gone."

"And she didn't know what he was talking about?"

"No," Jay said. "Neither do I."

"Hmm," Dean said.

We put down our little coffee cups and stood up.

"I'm going to go check the bedroom," Dean said.

"I'll wait down for you here," Jay said, and looked back out the window at that big yard, the pool, the volleyball net sagging in on itself. All that stuff. Funny how empty the things money can buy seem when the things it can't are gone.

6

Dean went into Brucie's room and stood holding the door until I came inside, and then he shut it behind me. It was unsaid but understood that my permission to be in the room with him was conditional on my shutting up and staying out of his way.

Maybe it's time to make something clear: Dean was a sickeningly good detective. It wasn't that he figured things out quickly. It was the exact opposite. It was that he steadily, deliberately didn't figure things out.

We always rush to make up a story to explain the world around us. Why we broke up with a girl, why we don't quit our job, why the other driver on the 401 is the dickhead, and not us. And pretty soon you stop seeing with your eyes the stuff that doesn't fit in with the story you made up in your head.

Dean didn't do that. He stripped away every story, every theory, every explanation, like layers of paint, until eventually the thing itself stood naked before him. He wasn't an easy guy to fool, our Dean. You should have seen him in California. It was epic.

"Hmm," Dean said, as he stood in the centre of the room with his hands in his pockets and his head tilted at a slight angle. "Hmm, hmm, hmm."

Big room, as you'd expect for an only child with a rich dad. The ceiling slanted down at an angle and the room itself was irregular. The bed was tucked in the corner in sort of a nook. Childish posters were on the wall, illustrations from *Treasure Island* and *Robin Hood*. A shelf of books (mostly comics collected in trade paperback form) stood next to a sturdy, expensive desk (antique maybe) bearing a sleek fire-engine-red laptop, as well as boxes of pencil crayons, brushes, paper and other artistic supplies and stacks of sketches of superheroes.

A picture of Brucie and Jay was on one of the shelves. I went over and picked it up. The kid looked like his dad, same sloped shoulders, husky physique, shy smile. He was taller though, broader, and had a terrible haircut. A big, goofy kid.

"Can you put that back please?" Dean asked.

I did and retreated back to the door.

Dean turned on the laptop and was confronted with a request for a password. He grunted.

"Can you take this in to someone and see if they can figure out how to get past this?"

"No problem," I said.

"You might have to do the same thing with the phone."

"I can but try," I said.

Dean carefully began to search the room. He started with the bed, pulling back the sheets and carefully checking the mattress. He looked at everything on the shelves, turning them over in his hands, sometimes even holding them up to his nose. That careful, present, look in his face. Under the bed he discovered a little filing system, which kept him busy for a while.

I knew it would bug him but I was getting restless so I started looking around. I opened the closet door. It was a big one – a walk in – but Brucie hadn't been a clothes guy. Half of the stuff on the hangers seemed to be old Halloween costumes. About seven or eight long rectangular boxes were sitting on the floor. I opened one, and saw that it was full of comic books, each one in a little sealed plastic bag with a cardboard backing. I flipped through them. They were organized alphabetically. Avengers, Black Panther, Captain America, Daredevil, and the Fantastic Four. And that was just Marvel. Another box I opened had DC: Aquaman, Batman, Detective Comics, Flash and Green Lantern.

One of the boxes was a little bigger and heavier than the others. The comic books inside were in hard plastic containers that were sealed shut. They made a clacking noise as I flipped through them. Each one had a label at the top, usually coloured blue, although a few were yellow or purple. The letters "CQC" were in the middle of the label, along with a bar code and a serial number, while a number between 1.0 and 9.9 was on the left and a hologram was on the right. These comics seemed older, like from the 70s and 80s. They were organized by date, instead of by name, and they were mostly issues of Amazing Spider-man.

The last box was empty, which struck me as odd. It had a title (Detective Comics #66) and a grade (9.0) but the seal had been broken and the comic was missing.

"Dean," I said, "check this out and tell me what you think."

I thought Dean sighed a little, but it could have been my imagination. He came over and asked: "What have you got?"

"Look," I said.

He studied the empty box. "What is this?"

"I don't know. Looks like Brucie was a comic guy. Big collection. Most of his comics are in plastic bags, but some of the older ones are in these fancy boxes. This one was empty."

"Good catch," Dean said.

Dean and I searched the room down to every last detail but we didn't find anything else of interest. I took the computer and Dean took some stuff from the file organizer, receipts and phone bills and such, but that was it.

Jay was still down in the solarium.

"We're going to go check out the bridge," Dean said.

"Okay," Jay said.

"Do you know Brucie's computer and phone passwords?"

"His computer, no," Jay said. "The phone is 7844."

Dean wrote that down. "One last thing. Do you know anything about this?" Dean said, and showed him the empty box.

Jay took it in his hands.

"That's odd," Jay said. "This is mine. Or at least, I think it is. I don't remember it being a 9. Brucie must have taken it from my collection downstairs. I wonder why it's out of the box."

"Can we check?" Dean asked.

So we went downstairs. The basement was semi-furnished, with foosball and air hockey tables. There were boxes and boxes of comic books, some in plastic sleeves, but most in clear plastic CQC cases. Jay flicked through them and found his copy of Detective Comics #66, the cover showing Batman on a tightrope while Robin hung from the hands of a giant clock. A man in a fedora was shooting a pistol at Batman from a rooftop. The words "Meet Two-Face" were printed at the top of the page.

"Yeah," Jay said. "See, look at this. My copy is only 6.5. I wonder where Brucie got that box from. That's probably about a $5,000 comic. I didn't see anything about comics on his most recent credit card statement."

"We'll take a look at some of his older statements and be in touch," Dean said. "Thanks Jay."

7

We took a short stroll down the leaf-lined street to the bridge. A raised sidewalk was on either side of the road, and good thing too, because the cars drove by awfully fast for a residential street. A thick concrete railing, about four feet high, separated us from the drop. Every ten feet or so there was a pillar that leaned away from the bridge at a bit of an angle.

We both looked down. It was odd to see the tops of trees.

"About 50 or 60 yards I guess," Dean said.
"You wouldn't necessarily die from that, would you?"
"No," Dean said, "but you easily could. It depends how you land. I've heard that anything over 30 feet is 50/50."

The Don River runs like a scar across the east side of the city, and sends up forested tendrils into different neighborhoods. Toronto isn't exactly nature tourist heaven, not like Calgary, or even Montreal, but it's criss-crossed by a lot of ravines, and there are plenty of nice parks. They aren't nicely manicured like Central Park or anything; they still feel a little wild. On a good day you might see a deer.

"Let's go down there and take a quick look," Dean said.

So, we headed back off the bridge and navigated our way down the steep slope, using the tree roots that stuck out of the ground like rungs or steps, and trying not to slip on the slick dirt. At the bottom it was dark and cold. The light filtered through the branches at a steep angle.

We didn't find anything of course, no dark patch on the ground or crucial little piece of evidence. Just the smell of urine and the usual graffiti, tags made in spray paint, so-and-so sucks cock.

"Hmm," Dean said.

We took the path back up into the sunlight.

"Ok," Dean said. "You busy tomorrow?"

"You mean Sunday? I'm watching football. "

"Okay, Monday."

"Right now, everything is clear."

"Well, I'm pretty jammed. How about this. Take a look at the credit card and bank statements and do a recon. See if you can figure out what all those charges are, and see if you can find when and where he bought that comic. Take a look at his phone. See who he was calling and who was calling him. And try to get into his computer. Hopefully he saved all his Facebook and email passwords. If not, I don't know. Maybe we can use the death certificate to get that info from someone."

"Yeah, we can figure that out," I said.

"I'm pretty busy at work, whatever Jay says, but let's plan to talk to the cop on Monday night. Sound good?"

"Great," I said.

"Okay," Dean said. "Let's go home for dinner."

8

Dean had a great house at Bloor and Jane, not far from the subway, with a lawn and a garden and everything.

"How'd you afford this? I asked.

"My wife paid for it," he said.

And then we opened the front door and Dean's wife came up to meet us.

"Terrell! How nice to see you!"

I shouldn't have been surprised. There was no reason to be surprised. Dean had worked for years in the adult film industry; it was not particularly surprising that he'd married a porn star. And Tina (who I'd actually only met once before) was a very wonderful person. Good looking too, with wide hips and big boobs and platinum blond hair. She was a bit heavier than when I'd seen her all those years ago, but she was over forty now. She still looked great.

It's hard for me to really remember what my initial impression was. I was surprised, definitely. And I was happy too. Like I said, Tina was one of those people who seem to have an inexhaustible store of kindness, who really thought the best of everyone. I think I remember feeling like maybe that was a great match, Dean with his inner darkness and his history of substance abuse, but being such a smart and great guy, with this nice person to understand him, to baby him, even.

But although I can't be sure, I think I remember being uneasy about it too. Was there something maybe a bit off about it? Dean, smart and cynical and sort of, I don't know, not all that lusty, with this big beautiful porn star, who although not a bimbo, necessarily, is maybe not really what you'd call an intellectual?

I'm not sure though. Maybe that's just hindsight. Maybe that's just me trying to make myself feel better about how things went down.

"Tina!" I said. "Holy shit!"

We embraced and I came inside.

"I haven't seen you in eight years," she said in her high, airy voice. "Crazy that you moved here too!"

"It's a small world," I said.

I was re-introduced to Krystal, now a teenager (which made me feel old) and I was respectfully shown baby Joseph, who was upstairs slumbering in his crib. That one was Dean's I gathered.

I sat in the back yard on an aluminum chair and drank a glass of wine with Dean.

"Don't talk about the detective work," he said. "I'm going to tell her. Just not tonight."

"Okay."

I was taking a sip of wine as Tina brought out a tray of hors d'oeuvres.

"Man," I said. "This wine is great. Was it expensive?"

"Eight bucks a bottle," Dean said.

"Isn't he awful?" Tina said. "He gets me all the time."

"Well, I like it," I said, and attacked the guacamole.

"Dean won't let me buy anything expensive unless I can tell the difference in a blind taste test."

"Harsh," I said. "Wait, no. Now that I think of it, that's pretty fair."

"Exactly!" Dean said.

"Terrell," she said, and leaned forward to slap my knee. "You're not helping."

"Blind experiments are the foundation of science," Dean said. "If a company is testing a drug, they give half the patients sugar pills, and they don't even tell the doctors which pills are real. But when a reviewer reviews a book, you can bet he knows who wrote it. When someone drinks wine, you can bet they know how much it cost or what picture it has on the label."

I noticed that Dean had already drunk half of his glass of wine. He took up the bottle and I thought he was going to refill his glass, but instead, he topped up Tina and I, even though we'd hardly drunk anything.

"I don't mind paying for anything if I can genuinely tell the difference," Dean said. "But it has to be for what's in the bottle, not what's on it."

"It's not even your money," Tina said.

"I love it," I declared as I took a handful of stuffed mushrooms. "I love it. I'm going to start doing that."

We chatted for a while, about how we liked Toronto, about people we used to know in California. Dean had a fancy charcoal barbeque with a separate container for woodchips and he was smoking an amazing-looking fish with the head still on. Eventually, the baby monitor started making noise and Tina left us.

"Seriously Dean," I said, "you've got it made here."

I looked around, admiring the spacious lawn, the beautiful flowers, the mature trees with their thick trunks and heavy branches. There was even a little Zen garden in the corner.

"Yeah, not bad," Dean said.

"I'm so happy for you," I said. And I swear, I meant it. "I was so worried about you when we split up. You didn't look good."

"Well," Dean said, "Tina really helped me turn it around. I was a good ways into NA when we started seeing each other. Then she helped me get through law school. I mean, I used my own money, but she supported me."

"Why'd you come up to Canada?"

"We both agreed it would be best if we got a change."

"Right," I said. I knew what he was talking about.

"The opportunity came up with Jay to come to Stewarts. I don't think I'll make partner but after a few years I should be able to get a good in-house job, or go to a smaller firm. Tina has a fair bit of money socked away. If we live off my salary for the next twenty years we'll be able to retire comfortably enough."

"Great," I said.

"What about you? Dean asked. "How'd you end up here?"

"Well, I moved here, then I met a girl, and we got married so I wouldn't have to go back to the States. I started doing the private eye thing. Then I got divorced."

"Sorry to hear that," he said.

"Well, what can you do? I'm okay with it, but she still hates me. I wish we could just talk. I think about her sometimes."

Dean didn't pry. He just swirled the rest of his wine around in his glass and stared at it like he was panning for gold. Eventually, after some careful consideration, he filled it halfway up.

"Two bottles in the house?"

"Yeah. Only one if we don't have guests. If we don't finish before I go to bed, I pour whatever's left down the drain. Otherwise it talks to me all night."

"Can people bring more booze with them? Say I want some gin?"

"Yes, but you have to take it with you when you leave."

"What if I stay over?"

"It goes down the sink."

"What if it's that expensive gin? Bombay Sapphire?"

"The sink."

"Harsh," I said.

"Also. Before you are allowed to buy expensive gin, you have to be able to distinguish it from Beefeater in a blind taste test."

I laughed. There was a comfortable pause. Then I asked:

"Dean, are you sure you're okay with this detective thing?"

For a minute, he didn't respond.

"Like the booze thing, right?" I said. "If you thought it would mess you up, you'd say no, right?"

Dean drank half of his glass of wine in one gulp, and gasped for breath a little, like a diver surfacing.

"I think it'll be okay," he said finally, which, of course, wasn't what I'd asked him.

9

On Sunday the Saints destroyed Chicago and it was good. I snacked on carrot sticks and hit the gym for the first time in five weeks. That was good too. Monday morning I drove into work feeling at peace with myself and the world. At my desk I sipped my coffee at my desk, and perused the Globe and Mail website.

I don't normally click on the business tab, but something guided my fingers there. And then bam!

OSC BROADENS INVESTIGATION TO INCLUDE EDENFREE BOARD LAWYER

Jason Goldstein of Stewart Brubaker questioned by OSC

"Holy shit," I said.

I read the first few lines of the article.

Following public outcry after the production of a controversial legal opinion, the OSC has included prominent corporate lawyer Jay Goldstein in its broadening investigation into the initial public offering of Edenfree.

The release of confidential e-mails showed that Royal Toronto Bank, who underwrote the IPO, believed the stock was significantly overvalued. Wes Nolan, a member of Edenfree's board, has also admitted that he believed that the shares were overvalued, but relied upon a legal opinion, provided by Goldstein, that he did not need to divulge his belief as it was not a "material fact."

The OSC said that they are still gathering information, and that the final decision to commence a proceeding has not yet been made. Goldstein and SBP did not comment for this story.

The general consensus in the legal world seems to be that Goldstein did nothing wrong.

"It looks terrible," said Gayle Penny, a senior partner with Waxman LLP. "But if you look at the definition of 'material fact', it probably doesn't include the opinion of a board member on the value of the stock, as long as all the information upon which that opinion is based was properly disclosed."

"Huh," I said.

I started getting to work on the tasks Dean had assigned me. A little bit before lunch I was disturbed by the sound of a woman crying and shouting. I couldn't make out what she was saying, but I didn't need to. It was Diana Burke, and she had already gone through two guys at our firm. By the sounds of things she was about to make it three for three.

After a little while the crying stopped and then there was a knock at my door. I only had a moment to process this before my door opened and Alan came in with Diana.

"Here he is," Alan was saying. "He's my best man. He just busted an insurance fraud case wide open. If he can't do it, no one can."

"Well," Diana said, "if that's the case I don't know why we didn't just use him to start with."

Oh man, oh man, I was thinking.

If you saw Diana Burke, you'd know her type: north of forty-five, lives in Rosedale or Forest Hill, dyes her hair, goes to the gym every day, knows how to spend money on clothes and make up, maybe she's even had a little work done. But in spite of that (or even maybe because of it) she looks old. Kind of dried out, or something.

Also, it didn't help that her makeup was smeared across her face by her tears and her eyes were blurry and unfocused.

"I'll leave you two to it," Alan said, and winked at me as he left, shutting the door behind him.

My office was not designed to receive visitors. I stood up and took my jacket off the one chair and motioned for her to sit down, which she did.

Her eyes roamed around, judging everything she saw, I imagined, till they fell on the framed quote hanging on the wall across from my desk. It said:

Men, you're the first Negro tankers to ever fight in the American Army. I would never have asked for you if you weren't good. I have nothing but the best in my Army. I don't care what color you are as long as you go up there and kill those Kraut sons of bitches. Everyone has their eyes on you and is expecting great things from you. Most of all your race is looking forward to you. Don't let them down and damn you, don't let me down!

If you need to find me I'll be in the lead tank.

George S. Patton

"That's an unusual quote," she said.

"My grandfather fought in that unit," I said. "He was a tank driver, and he admired Patton very much."

"You know Patton was a dreadful racist," she said.

I just smiled at this. Yeah, I did know that. Still, my grandpa had always liked him. He said you always knew where you stood with The Old Man. Since then I've always thought: fuck pretending to be someone else. People like you the most when they know who you are.

"Well," I asked, "how can I help you?"

"You know what I want," she said. "I need to you to catch my husband with whatever whore he's seeing."

"You're sure he's cheating on you?" I said.

"Yes," she replied. "Of course I'm sure."

"How do you know?" I said.

"A woman always knows," she said. "I just can't prove it yet."

I could hear Dean saying in my mind: *If we couldn't prove it, by definition we didn't know.*

I wanted to say: *this is nutty, and so are you. Go away and get yourself together. Do some yoga and then drink a five dollar tea or something.*

But she was a payer. If she wanted to keep burning through detectives, that was her prerogative.

"Well okay," I said. "I'll get the details from the file and call you if I have any questions?"

"All right," she said.

"Unless you have anything more to add?"

"Read the file first," she said.

"Okay. Well, I'll be in touch soon, Mrs. Burke."

"Thank you," she said.

I showed her out and spent about an hour reviewing her file. It was pretty detailed. The husband's first name was Anthony. The pictures showed he was a big, fleshy dude. Olive-skinned, with dark, curly hair, and a cruel face. Looked kind of like the Emperor Nero.

He and his wife had both been born into money. Business had been good and now they were richer than ever. First they'd done some Internet thing, then she'd started a restaurant in Yorkville (which had failed) and he'd started a private art gallery at Church and Front (which had apparently prospered).

Surveillance logs for went on for weeks and weeks. The Burkes lived the typical Toronto high life. House in Forest Hill? Check. Cottage on Lake Muskoka? But of course. Trips abroad? You know it. None of us had ever caught him doing anything. Apparently he was pretty good at knowing when he was being watched. My buddy D.J. had faithfully recorded how Burke had come up to him in his car while he was on surveillance, knocked on his window, and given him a box of cinnamon buns.

I didn't get too worried about that. I get paid by the hour whether I get made or not. And I love cinnamon buns.

I spent the afternoon working on the stuff for Dean, and when my Blackberry buzzed, I headed over to visit him.

10

Unusually for a junior lawyer (still less a student) Dean's office was scrupulously tidy, and photos hung on the walls. Tina, his kids, some older pictures of what I assumed was his family, and, holy shit! A great shot of Dean and I in the badlands of Arizona.

"Did you just put that up now?" I asked.

"No man," Dean said. "I've had that up a while."

"No way!" I laughed. I was super happy about that. "Look at us. Oh, man. Look how skinny I was back then."

"Pull up a chair," Dean said. "This cop leaves work at four, I hope we catch him."

We did. He picked up after a couple of rings.

"Detective Aston," he said

"Hi Detective," Dean said. "This is Dean Mann, I'm an attorney, and I'm here with Terrell Delacroix, a private detective."

"You're not a lawyer," Aston said. "You're a student."

Dean laughed.

"You're right."

"That can get you in trouble with the law society, you know."

"Thanks for the heads up," Dean said. "So, as I said, my boss, Jay Goldstein, has hired Mr. Delacroix to look into his son's death."

"Right."

"So we're hoping to talk about your investigation."

"You want to know about my investigation?" Aston said. "Here's what happened. I got the call when the joggers found this poor kid's body. I was on the scene fifteen minutes after he was found. The constables had already isolated the area. Now right away, it was obvious this was a straight jumper case. We get them all the time. There's one jumper a week in the city, even after they put up the Luminous Veil on the Prince Edward Viaduct. But, you'll be happy to hear, we did everything by the book. Right from the beginning Goldstein was on my case, and so I didn't miss a trick. We had forensics go over the path, and the bridge above, with a fine tuned comb. We even dusted the bridge for finger prints. I know you watch CSI, so you think we do that all the time. Let me tell you: we do not."

"Right," Dean said, as he jotted quick, almost illegible notes on a green pad of paper.

"So what do I do? Astn continued. "Well, I start by talking to the parents. They tell me: no way Brucie killed himself! He's such a happy boy and he had so much to live for! Oh, but, by the way, he'd been very troubled recently, and over the past few days he'd barely come out of his room."

"Right," Dean said.

"So I talk to everyone on the street. No one saw anything. I talk to all this kid's friends. Does he have any enemies? Has he been in trouble? No, everyone likes him, he'd never kill himself! But no one's seen him in a while. He's been keeping to himself and he's been upset the past few days. Not answering his phone."

"Right," Dean says.

"I search his room. No note, but nothing suspicious either. We look at his Facebook. Nothing. We look at his phone. A bunch of weird calls from disposable phones, but otherwise nothing. I go up and down the street and ask if anyone saw anything. Nothing. Then the fingerprint report comes back. We found a complete set of Brucie's prints on the inside of the rail of the bridge. But get this: they were upside-down. So either he walked up, turned his arms around and pressed his fingers there, or ..."

"Or he was hanging from the other side," Dean said.

"Right. And then the coroner's report comes back. No signs of a struggle. Cause of death, the fall. That's that. I tried to tell that to your boss, and he hit the roof. Made noises about suing me. For what? I don't know. You're the lawyer, you tell me. We had every right to close that case as a suicide. But we left it open. For a while Mr. Goldstein called me, said I should keep investigating. I'm like:

investigate what? We have no more leads. You have a lead, then give it to me. That was the last I heard from him."

"Right," Dean said. "Did you hear anything about debt? Money problems? When you spoke to Brucie's friends?"

"No," Aston said. "Did he have money problems?"

"Well, maybe," Dean said.

"What makes you think that?"

"It's just an angle we're looking into."

"Well, there's your motive for suicide," Aston said. "Money problems? Credit card debt? Man. I guess he just couldn't tell his dad. Kids. Everything's so serious to them. Permanent solution to a temporary problem. Kid kills himself over money with a dad that rich? You think he wouldn't clear those cards to get his kid back?"

"No kidding," Dean said. "Can we get a copy of your file?"

"Sure," Aston said. "But you've got to do a freedom of information request. I don't just give that stuff out."

"Right."

"Look, Mr. Mann," Aston said. "I work hard at my job. I'm passionate about it. Okay? This is a suicide. If your boss can't accept it, sucks for him, and sucks for you."

"Thanks," Dean said.

"We left this a suspicious death and not a suicide, despite that we have officially exhausted all avenues of investigation. You find anything you think we should be aware of, then send it over. I'm not opposed to working on this more. I just don't see anything more to do. You get stuff on this debt angle, let me know."

"Hey, thanks," Dean said. "Will do. You've been really candid with me and I appreciate it."

"All right. Talk to you later, Mr. Mann. You too Mr. Delacroix."

"Bye," Dean said, and pushed the disconnect button.

"Do you think we should take him some of this stuff about the debt?" I asked.

"Why? What have you got for me?"

"Lots," I said.

I got out my file with all my notes.

"For starters, I did the recon of the credit card statements and the bank statements," I said. "There are eight $2,000 charges to the same Moneris machine."

"What for?"

"That's the thing, I don't know. I guess we'll know more once Jay hears back from the credit card company."

"Okay," Dean said. "Anything else?"

"There was a $9,000 charge to Paradise Comics on the Visa on July 18," I said. "That could be when he bought the comic. There's also small charges to Paradise Comics most weeks before that, either on the credit card, or the bank statements. Usually around $20 every Wednesday."

"Okay," Dean said, leaning back, pressing his finger tips together in front of his mouth. "So what do you spend $2,000 on eight times? My guess: drugs, gambling, blackmail. Or sex."

"Speaking of sex," I continued, "the first $2,000 charge is in early June. But when I cross-referenced that with his bank records, I saw that he made a withdrawal at the ATM at the Brass Rail on May 20. Two hundred dollars."

"Uh oh," Dean said. "He shouldn't be in there at seventeen years old."

"In terms of the phone," I continued, going through my notes. "There was lot of activity the day he died, and the day before. He got six calls from one number, five of which were missed, one which was received. I tried calling it. It's disconnected. If Aston says it's from a disposable phone, I believe him. Then Brucie got a call from another number, which he picked up, around midnight on August 30."

"Right before he died," Dean said.

"Yep," I replied. "There's also a few outgoing calls to the maid. I called her and confirmed what Jay said. Brucie phoned her and asked about a black box. She said he was frantic, almost accusing her. She said it was really unlike him."

Dean leaned way back in his chair and looked at the ceiling.

"So, with all due respect to Detective Aston, something weird was going on," Dean said.

"Yeah," I said.

"But," Dean said, "nothing that really points to anything but suicide."

"No," I said. "Especially with all the forensic work they did."

"Well, here's the thing," Dean said. "It's very difficult to spot signs of a struggle on someone who has fallen to their death. When you hit the ground from that height, everything's a mess. And when you only find the body six, eight hours later? Blood and bruising everywhere, lots of swelling. Very tough. That's why Soviet agents in Europe used to assassinate people by throwing them out windows. Defenestration, they called it."

"You really think someone killed Brucie?"

"I don't know," Dean said. "I don't have enough information to think anything. But even if we could shed some light on why Brucie committed suicide, it might make Jay feel better."

"Yeah," I said.

"I'd like to talk to these comic guys," Dean said. "I mean, Brucie is in the middle of all these other money problems, and then he drops $9,000 on one comic? I don't get it."

"Me neither," I said.

"Well," Dean said, "let me know if you get anything off that computer. I better get back to this due diligence."

"Good luck," I said. "I'm going to catch some football."

11

Tuesday morning started with a little surveillance. I sat in the windowless dark of the back of a white panel van, looking at a glowing computer screen. That crazy Burke lady had let us bug their phones and put cameras in certain rooms of their house, so I was able to watch our friend Anthony doing up his shoes in the mudroom of their fancy Forest Hill home. When he jogged outside the front door, I flipped to the external camera and watched him start his run. Every morning, the logs said, he went for a jog down into Sir Winston Churchill Park.

While I waited for him to come back, I reviewed the logs. He didn't have much of a fixed schedule. Every day he roamed around the city, visiting clients and artists, going to shows, attending functions. His gallery was right downtown. Not only that, he also went to New York and London every month, and if he wanted to sleep with women in those places, it would be tough for me to catch him.

When he left for the day I followed him, pretty far back. I was more worried about getting made than losing him. Diana said he was going to his gallery at Church and Front and if he didn't show up there that told me something in and of itself. Surveillance is all about taking what they give you, letting the whole situation speak to you. Dean taught me that.

Anyway, I did manage to keep up with him almost all the way downtown. His car ducked down into an underground lot, so I parked illegally to stay on the street and then walked into the Second Cup on the southeast corner of Church and Front.

The day was warm and the big windows were open, so I sat with a peanut butter and chocolate ice drink and waited for Anthony. The intersection was y-shaped, where two one-way streets going different directions merged together. Canada's own

Flatiron Building stood on the west side of Church, a building that sharpened to a point where the two streets joined. The St. Lawrence Market, a big brick warehouse filled with yuppie grocery stores, was just to the east. Further east you got to the Distillery District, one of the biggest collections of nineteenth century buildings in North America. Overall, it was a nice neighborhood for a gallery, with all the brick and beam stuff.

Anthony appeared at the far street corner. I liked his suit. It was shiny and colourful, but not tacky. It looked like money. In person, Anthony gave off a slightly imperious air, but when an Asian kid trying to take a picture of the Flatiron Building backed into him, he just smiled at the apology, and when a bum stopped him for changed he not only gave him a buck but spoke with him easily for a moment.

Lord of the castle, are you? I thought. I get it.

He walked past me, further south down Church. Anthony's gallery was actually below ground level. Windows you had to crouch down to look through. There was no way to watch what he was doing. If I go in there, a big black dude that knows nothing about art, what's he going to think?

I got up and walked south on Church, casually heading to my car on the Esplanade. A sandwich board stood next to the door of the gallery. There was a show for an artist named Anna Herowicz coming up. Refreshments would be served, which was quite a happy coincidence, because I love refreshments. Maybe I would take that opportunity to poke around.

My Blackberry buzzed as I got back to the van. Our tech dude had cracked the computer. Good times. I picked up a yellow parking ticket from under the wipers and put the van in gear.

12

I spent two hours screwing around on Brucie's bright red computer (which had a big glowing alien head on the back) before I called Dean.

"Good news," I said. "Passwords in Facebook and Gmail were automatically saved. Once we got Windows up and running, everything was there."

"Great," Dean said. "Got anything for me?"

"Nothing on Facebook except for RIP messages. I left a post with my phone number, asking anyone who has information to call me or the police."

"Okay," Dean said. "Don't mention my name. I don't want people at the firm talking."

"I didn't. Anyway, Gmail was more interesting."

"How so?"

"So Brucie gets an e-mail from Paradise Comics every weekend, usually on Saturday. It's just a list of the comics that come out that week, Brucie e-mails back, says which ones he wants, and I guess they put them aside for him. So that explains the weekly charges on his credit card. But two weeks before Brucie bought the expensive Batman comic he got an e-mail from Paradise Comics. The e-mail says 'Hey Brucie, I checked your list, looks like I can get two of them. Detective Comics #66 and Incredible Hulk #181. CQC numbers are below. Let me know which one you'd like.' The e-mail also gives the CQC numbers. No e-mail back from Brucie. I looked but I can't find the list that Brucie sent them."

"All right," Dean said.

"But it gets better," I went on. "I went a little further back. The day after Brucie went to the Brass Rail in May, he sent an e-mail to someone at your firm. A guy named Rob Guilliam."

"Rob?" Dean said.

"The e-mail says, quote: 'Dude, you've got to send me the number for that girl's agency. I'm going nuts here! Hook a brother up!' Rob e-mails him back, five minutes later, but from his personal account. He says, quote: 'Don't e-mail me about this at my work account. Also: why don't we hold off on this for a little while. Think it over a bit. She's not going anywhere.' Brucie then e-mails him back, but at his work account again. He says, quote, 'Don't give me that bullshit! You said you had the info, come on man! Give me the number!' No more emails to or from Mr. Guilliam."

"Huh," Dean said. "Get down here and we'll talk to him. Then we'll head up to Paradise Comics."

Dean met me in the lobby at Stewarts and escorted me down the hall. The door to Rob's office was open and so Dean knocked and we entered.

"Boys!" Rob said. "Good to see you."

"Hey Rob," Dean said. "This is Terrell, the private investigator I told you about."

"Take a seat," Rob said. "Close the door behind you, though, would you?"

Rob was an example of a type you actually see quite frequently at law firms: the smart jock. A former football player at McGill, Rob was tall and very broad across the chest. The suit he wore was neat but not extravagant and his hair was cut very short. The kind of guy who was always talking about sports and calling you dude but read the Economist and could tell you what the housing crisis was all about.

A signed, framed Daniel Alfredsson jersey hung on the wall. The window had a lovely view of the 44th floor of the Scotia Plaza, directly across the street.

"So anyway," Dean said, "Like I said on the phone ..."

"Look," Rob interrupted, "I know why you're here. Okay? I'm actually pretty relieved. It was getting to me. I should have told someone about this stuff earlier. But who was I supposed to tell? This is killing Jay. I didn't think it would make it any easier for him."

"Right," Dean said.

"How did you find out?"

"Well, we got into his e-mails."

"That little shit," Rob said, and shook his head. "Poor bastard. He was a great kid."

"So what happened?" Dean asked.

"The second Thursday in May," Rob started, in a lower voice, "me and Gilles and a bunch of guys took some of the students out to the Duke after work. We ended up getting shittered and turned out it was one of their birthdays so we all went up to the Rail. And when I get out of my cab, who do I see walking up the street all by his lonesome? Brucie."

"How'd you know him?" Dean asked.

"He's always at firm events, things like that," Rob said. "He was on my curling team last year. Anyway, he had some bullshit, McLovin-style fake ID with him and I slipped the bouncer a twenty and I got him in. He was like a kid in a candy store, just staring at everything. I sat him down, got him a Corona, everyone was laughing fit to bust."

Rob looked at us defensively.

"I mean, he was only seventeen, or whatever. But I was going to strip clubs in Montreal when I was eighteen. And he didn't seem like the type to bug out."

"Sure," Dean said.

"Well, then this super hot chick comes out. I mean, all the strippers are pretty hot, but this one's just absurd. Nuts. Like airbrushed, but in real life. Her name's Tanya."

At the sound of that name, I must have jerked in my chair a little. Right away I looked over at Dean, who had not reacted at all.

"You know her?" Rob asked.

"No, we don't know her," Dean said, giving me a look. "Go ahead."

"Well, Brucie, he's just such a big kid. When she's on stage his jaw just hit his chest. He was blown away. We were all laughing at him. Now I actually know this stripper. I don't want to give you the idea I'm in the strip club every day, but I was there for a bachelor's party a couple months ago and I know that one of my buddies was so taken with her that he got contact info for her from somewhere. I think I said that when she was doing her dance. Brucie was staring so hard at that girl I wasn't even sure he'd heard me. I mean seriously. It looked like he was doing damage to his eyeballs. That was how hard he was staring at this girl."

"Right," Dean said.

"So Brucie goes back for a private dance," Rob continued, "until she finally kicks him out and he gets thrown out of the strip club entirely. I guess he was trying to get her to marry him back there and she finally just said, 'you are just a boy,' or whatever. Then the rest of us all got kicked out too. We were wasted."

"Did you see Brucie again that night?"

"No, Rob said, "and even in my drunken state I was pretty worried about that. Bouncers are assholes and for all I knew they totally kicked the shit out of him. Or he could have got hit by a car, or whatever. I didn't know what to do."

"And the next morning?"

"The next morning I get this e-mail, at my fucking work account, asking me for the girl's details. So I wrote him back from my Gmail through my Blackberry and just said, hey dude, let's think about this. The little prick e-mails me back at work, again, and so I call him. He threatens me on the phone."

"Explicitly?"

"No, not in so many words, but he just kept saying, we were there together, and he needs to get it from me. So finally I said, Brucie, do your worst. That's what I said. I mean, this is my career, but if he's going to play that card now, for all I know he's going to play it tomorrow. I figured I had to put a stop to it. So I just said: no way. You want to tell your dad, go ahead."

"And you didn't hear anything more about it?"
"No. I figured he'd be in as much trouble as I would, so he kept it to himself."

"When was the next time you saw him?"
"Never," Rob replied. "I never saw him again before he died. Look man, I am so sorry. I want you to know that. The way he was asking for that girl. Something was off about it. He was obsessed, even though he'd only seen her for like two seconds. I should have gone straight to Jay. But I didn't know what would happen."

"And then after it happened," Dean said, "what's the point of telling him?
"Yeah," Rob said. "Like I said, I'm glad to tell you."
"Thanks Rob," Dean said. "If you're sure that's all you know, I think I can probably keep your name out of it."
"Well, if you can, great. If you can't, you can't." Rob said. "Do what you gotta do."
He sighed.
"Fucked up man," Rob said. "His only kid."

"Yeah," Dean said.
Rob shook his head, and then looked at me.
"So what're you letting him do all the questioning for?" he said in a more boisterous voice. "You're the investigator!"
"I'm supervising," I said.
Rob laughed at that, and then turned back to his computer as we left his office.

13

We rode the subway up to Lawrence and then started walking up Yonge. Paradise Comics was about one third of the way to York Mills and so Dean lit a cigarette.

"Don't tell Tina," he said.

"Does she think you quit?" I asked.

"I did quit," he said.

I changed the subject.

"I just about had a heart attack when he said the girl's name was Tanya," I said.

Dean just grunted.

"Man," I said.

We were quiet the rest of the walk.

Paradise Comics was a long, narrow store. The walls were lined with graphic novels, softcover trade paperbacks and hardcovers, and those expensive action figures they make for college students. At the back wall there was a smaller shelf with this week's new releases, all the slim little comics each in its own plastic bag with a board, just like in Brucie's boxes. The sales counter was on the left side of the room. It was made of glass, and inside there were some older comics in those hard plastic boxes with numbered grades in the top right. A red headed guy in his twenties was behind the counter. "Can I help you sir?" he asked.

"Yeah," Dean said. "My name's Dean Mann. This is Terrell Delacroix. We've been retained by Jay Goldstein to look into what happened to his son."

"Uh," the clerk said. "Hold on. Let me go get Peter."

He went down the stairs behind him to the basement and we were left alone in the store a while. I tapped the glass counter.

"Check it out," I said. "X-men from 1970."

"You want to get one?"

"No thanks man," I said. "I don't know how much they are, but I'm sure it's too much for a book I don't even get to read."

The clerk came back up the stairs with a slightly older blond man with an earring in one ear.

"Hey, you guys are here about Brucie?" he said.

"Yeah," Dean said. "My name is Dean and this is Terrell."

"I thought it was suicide," Peter said.

"Well, it's not clear," Dean said. "It's still technically considered a suspicious death. We're just looking into things a bit. Do you mind if we ask you a few questions?"

"Ask away," Peter said. "I feel terrible about what happened. Jay's been my customer for 20 years."

"Really?" I said.

"Sure," Peter said. "Jay Goldstein is a big Toronto collector. His collection's insured at a million dollars I think. And Brucie was a member here."

"What does that mean?" Dean asked.

"Just that he gets a discount and we set aside his books for him every week. He hadn't been in for a few weeks in a row. I figured he'd just gone to school early. We were going to keep his books for him till he came back for American Thanksgiving. I heard about what happened from some of his old high school buddies. I couldn't believe it. He was like my happiest customer."

"Brucie was a great guy," the red haired clerk chimed in.

"So you don't know anything about something that could have been getting him down?" Dean asked.

"No, no."

"He didn't mention any women problems or anything?"

Peter assumed a somewhat ironic expression. "My clientele generally don't run into a lot of women problems."

I laughed.

"Right," Dean said. "Well, back in July, did you sell Brucie a $9,000 comic?"

"Yeah," Peter said. "Detective Comics #66. First appearance of Two-Face. Brucie said it was a present for Jay. I thought Jay already had that one, but I guess not. Also a pretty expensive present. It was weird, but whatever. For Jay's kid, I would have taken it back, as long as it was still in the box."

"Can you tell me how that went down?"

"He came in here with a list of books he was looking for, asked me to check what I had, and to send him the CQC numbers because he wanted to check the grading notes."

"Do you still have the list he gave you?"

"No, sorry."

"All right. Can you tell me what you mean by checking the grading notes?"

"Well," Peter said, "when CQC grades a comic, three graders take notes on the condition of the comic. Slight tear on page four, water damage on page 18. That kind of thing. So you know what you're getting. Then CQC averages the three scores, and that's how you get the final score you see on the box. So if it says 8.5, could be that one grader gave it an 8.0, one 8.5 and one 9.0. But usually the scores are closer together than that."

"And you can look up the grading notes online if you have the number?"

"Sure," Peter said.

"Why does it matter whether it's an 8.5 or a 9.0 if you don't take it out of the box?" I asked.

"Well," Peter said. "Let me give you an extreme example. AF 15, okay?"

"What?" I said.

"Amazing Fantasy 15," Peter said. "First appearance of Spiderman."

"Right," I said.

"A 9.4 will sell for around $250,000," Peter said.

"That's nuts," I said.

"A 9.6, though, sold for $1,000,000."

"What?" I shouted.

"Whoa, hold on," Dean said. "So 0.2 is $750,000?"

"Sure, for that one comic."

"Okay, back up," Dean said. "Who is CQC?"

"Comic Quality Certification," Peter said. "They validate and grade comics. So you send in your comic ..."

"How?" Dean interrupted.

"You have to do it through someone with an account. So for example, I have an account. So if you dig around in your attic, and find a copy of AF 15, you bring it in to me and I send it to them."

"Where are they?"

"Sarasota, Florida."

"Okay. And I pay a flat fee?"

"How much you pay depends on the value of the comic. More expensive comics cost more but get graded faster. CQC doesn't want them sitting around, for insurance purposes."

"Okay. Then what? You're saying three graders look at it?"

"Graders look at it, they make sure it's authentic, they make sure it hasn't been restored, they pick a number for its quality, they seal it up in a special box, and then they send it back to you. And now you've got your comic, and it's preserved and so on, with an official grade from CQC."

"So it's easier to trade on the secondary market?"

"Exactly," Peter said.

"But, I mean, this company," Dean said, "I find AF 15 in my attic. Okay? It's smushed between two encyclopedias so it's in good condition. I send it down to Florida. Whether they give it a 9.4 or 9.6 is worth 750 large to me?"

"Yep," Peter said.

"Are they accountable? Can you appeal?"

"Appeal what?" Peter said. "It's just their opinion. Read the back of the box. You don't like it, take it out of the box."

"But then in practice you can't sell it if it's out of the box?"

"Depends how much you want for it."

"How long has CQC been around?"

"Ten years. They did the same thing with coins for a long time, and they had a trading card business for a while too, I think."

"And you've been in business for twenty?"

"Twenty years this year, yes."

"Have they been good for the industry?"

"Yes, absolutely," Peter said. "No doubt. Because it lets more people participate in the market. Let me tell you a story. I have another long term client. Richer than Jay. He bought a Detective Comics 27. First appearance of Batman, for $100,000. He sent it down to CQC, came back with the purple label of death. 9.4, but restored."

"So if it's restored it's worth less?"

"I sold that comic for him for $8,000."

"What the fuck," I said. I couldn't contain myself. "It's the same fucking comic."

"Doesn't matter," Peter said. "Anyway, that client said he's never buying a comic over a thousand dollars without me again, because he can't tell whether something's been touched up, just a little. And CQC gives everyone access to having a guy like me. You can buy with confidence. You can buy a comic over the internet from a guy in California. He just puts up the grade, the CQC number, and you know what you're getting."

"And you trust them?" Dean said.

"Sure, because you see them around at all the conventions. One time, at the beginning, I went over to their table at Comic Con over because I wasn't happy about a score I got on one of my books. So the guy said, oh, the president's busy, he'll be right over. Whatever, I thought. But sure enough, the president came over to my booth in fifteen minutes and talked to me about my score. They're very open. They'll tell you exactly why you got the score you did. It's very easy to get the information."

"Does CQC have any competitors?" Dean asked.

"No, not really. There's this one other company, but you can't trust them. One of my customers bought a book they graded at 9.2. If it had a grade from CQC, even if that grade was a little lower, it would have been worth more. So he sent it to CQC, and it came back restored. Value went down to nothing. The other company missed the restoration and my buddy relied on their ranking and he got screwed. In this business, trust is everything. CQC has it and right now, nobody else does."

"Doesn't CQC ever get fooled?" I asked.

"Yeah, sometimes. There was a big scandal with this guy Chuck Swinburne back in 2005. Basically, what happened is one year an AF 15 with a score of 8.8 came up for sale at Heritage, one of the big online auction houses. Heritage puts up these crazy high quality scans up on their website. So that comic sold. A few years go by, and another AF 15 comes up for sale at auction. Only this one is graded 9.2. But some dudes online figure out by looking at the scans that it's the same comic. Because these old comics, you can tell. Just the position of the staples or a little wrinkle or a crease or something. And so: how'd the same comic get a better score like that? Turns out it had been restored with micro-trimming."

"What?" Dean said.

"Just trimming the edges of the comic by a tiny little amount," Peter said. "Shaving off tiny bits to make the edges straighter and smoother. It can make that little difference that's worth a lot of money. Anyway, it was such a good job it had fooled CQC. So the book got traced back to Swinburne and it was a big scandal. CQC offered to re-grade all the books he'd ever submitted for free. And Swinburne is out of the hobby now. If he went to a convention he'd get attacked."

"Can I just say that's nuts?" I said.

"Yeah," Peter said. "It's kind of nuts."

"First, who wants comic books if you can't even look at them?" I said. "Second, what the hell is 0.2 quality difference worth? Especially if you can't take them out of the box? Why does it matter so much if it's restored?"

"Look man," Peter said. "Your guess is as good as mine. But the money involved has really gone up with CQC now. With the trust that they've been able to bring to the hobby, a lot more people are participating. But they aren't making more vintage comics. So prices go up."

"CQC makes a lot of money?" Dean asked.

"Presumably." Peter said. "But it's a private company, so who knows?"

"Okay," Dean said.

Dean opened his briefcase and took out the empty box.

"Recognize this?" he asked.

Peter flipped it around in his hands.

"Yeah, where's the comic?"

"We found it empty in Brucie's room."

"Empty?" Peter asked.

"Yeah," Dean said. "We don't know where the comic is, or who stole it."

"Stole it?" Peter said. "You said you found the empty box in Brucie's room?"

"Yeah," Dean said.

"Well, why would they leave the box behind if they stole it? It loses a lot of its value."

"You could report it stolen though, right?" I said. "If you kept a record of the CQC number?"

"Yeah," Peter said. "But even so, I don't understand why a thief would leave the box behind. Why wouldn't he just take the comic out of the box when he got home? I think Brucie must have taken it out himself."

"But why would he do that?" Dean asked.

"Hold on," Peter said. "Let me check something."

Peter shooed the red-haired clerk away from the computer and logged onto the CQC website. In a moment he'd pulled up the grading notes of the comic Brucie had bought.

"See, this is interesting," Peter said. "Look."

He turned the monitor so we could see what he was looking at: a scan of a type-written document with three columns of point-form notes.

"Looks like one guy graded it 9.0, one 9.2 and one 8.8."

"Is that usual?" Dean asked.

"No," Peter said. "It's not unheard of, but it's not usual, no."

"So how much is the price spread on this comic?" Dean asked. "How much difference does 0.2 make?"

"On this comic?" Peter asked. "I would say if a 9.0 is $9,000, an 8.8 is around $2,000, and a 9.2 would be $20,000. At least."

"Holy shit," Dean said. "So if he resubmits it, and the average goes up ..."

"He'd make at least ten grand," Peter confirmed. "To tell you the truth, now that I think of it, I was thinking of resubmitting this one myself, before Brucie bought it. There's a risk of course. It could go down instead of up."

"You might want to give it a little helping," the red haired clerk laughed.

"Helping?" Dean said. "Like restoration?"

"Well," Peter said, "there are things you can do that don't count as restoration. Pressing is a good example. You basically iron the wrinkles out of the comic. Some people online say that counts as restoration, but CQC doesn't. I mean, how could it? If I put a comic underneath a heavy book, am I restoring it? Of course not."

"Brucie never told you he was going to resubmit it, though, right?" Dean asked.

"No, he said it was for his dad. I remember that."

"And he obviously didn't resubmit it through this store?"

"No. No way."

"Hmm," Dean said. "Okay. One last thing: does CQC keep a record of who submits what comic?"

"Well," Peter said, "it's not available to the public. And as you can see, it's not on the grading notes. But yeah, I bet they've got something somewhere. Which account it was submitted through, anyway."

"Can you guess what I'm going to ask you next?" Dean said, smiling a little.

"You want to know the account this comic was originally submitted through?"

"Yes sir."

"For Jay," Peter said. "Anything."

"Thanks Peter," Dean said. He set his business card down. "We really appreciate it."

We stopped at Starbucks on our way back to the subway. Dean got an unsweetened iced coffee and I got a pumpkin spice latte.

"What do you think?" I asked.

"I don't know," Dean said as we ambled south.

We were coming up on the edge of Sherwood Park, part of the same network of parks and ravines where Brucie had died. From here, you could take wooded trails all the way down to the lake.

"I bet you he resubmitted that bad boy," I said. "That's why he checked the grading scores before he bought it. We know he had money trouble."

"Well, if he resubmitted it, we should be able to figure out where," Dean said. "Check the bank statements and the credit card statements again. If nothing comes up, start making calls."

"You got it boss," I said. "What do we do now?"

"Let's go to the rippers," he said.

14

But first we went to Jack Astors and sat on the patio overlooking Dundas Square. Dean drank virgin Caesars and I had Bud Light Lime. We chatted about basketball, both of us complaining about the lockout, while the sun went down. During the conversation Dean's phone buzzed and he picked it up and looked at it. His expression was very casual as he set it back down again. It's not an excuse, but when I grabbed it to read what it said, I wasn't expecting to see anything personal.

Hey sexy turtle, when do I get to suck u off??

I dropped the phone as if I'd been scalded.

"Dude," Dean said,"what the fuck?"

"Sorry man!" I said. "I didn't know.

"Well, what did you think it was?"

"I don't know, I said.

And it's true, I hadn't known. I do that all the time, look at people's e-mails, their texts, whatever. I'm a curious guy. But what alarmed me was my memory of Dean's face when he'd seen that text. The blank look. Like he was looking at a grocery list or a note from his boss. I knew they'd been married a few years, and she'd had his kid, and romance doesn't last forever. I know that one better than anybody. But there was something off about it, something that worried me.

"Sexy turtle?" I said, trying to change the subject.

Dean smiled.

"Peep not through keyholes," he said, "lest ye be vexed."

"Hey," I said, "you know, we don't have to go to the strippers tonight."

"No, tonight's a good night. Work is finally under control."

"Okay," I said.

The Brass Rail was in a little mini red-light area, just north of Zanzibar's (another strip club) and a sex toy emporium. Pictures of women, bronzed and pneumatic, were all over the front entrance. The bouncer nodded us through and we checked in our coats with the girls.

"Is Tanya on tonight?" Dean asked.

"Ten pm" the girl said with a bright smile. "But she's in the Upper Rail."

I always feel this big urge to flirt with the coat check girls, the waitresses, and the bartender in strip clubs. Everyone but the strippers.

"All right," Dean said.

We had to pay an extra ten bucks each, and then we climbed the purple carpeted stairs into the dark with the deep bass thudding all around us. We passed through another door into the Upper Rail. It was mostly empty. Just one table of dudes in suits and then a few pervs up on perverts row. An Asian girl was bending over and gripping her ankles on the stage, surrounding by mirrors, so that every square inch of her skin was on display. She slowly traced her hands up her legs. AC/DC was blaring over the sound system.

We sat down. Every few minutes a girl would wander up and sit in my lap, and I'd flirt with them, until they finally asked me whether I wanted a dance. When I said no, they'd leave. Only one or two bothered making a pass at Dean. He had a polite way of looking at them that was completely absent of desire.

Mostly we watched the baseball game, which was on the TV above the stage. One girl after another got up and danced, with the sleazy announcer saying things to the effect of: "Give it up for Jessica!"

Dean and I had pretty much run out of things to say to each other and private investigating is thirsty work. By ten o'clock I was pretty drunk, while Dean was stone sober, drinking coke and ignoring the dirty looks from the waitresses.

Around 9:45 I noticed someone new at the bar. Something about him wasn't quite right. He was a black guy, slender, with cornrows, wearing a plain black turtleneck and jeans. Often I caught him looking at us like he could tell we didn't belong.

A little bit before ten, a girl came and sat in my lap. She was older than me, I guess, good body, tight, with freckles on her nose. We were talking about a lot of different things, California mostly, where she'd lived for some time. Her name, she said, was Chantelle.

"Who's that dude at the bar?" I asked her at one point. "Does he work here?"

"No," Chantelle said. "He hangs out with one of the girls here."

"A boyfriend?" I asked.

"No," Chantelle said, "it's complicated."

And then the dirtbag announcer (I swear to god, it is the same guy at every strip club in the world) came over the announcing system, booming out in his weird robotic voice, "Gentlemen, let me hear you put your hands together for the lovely and beautiful Tanya, give it up for Tanya!"

And she came down the stairs carefully in her big red heels, dressed only in her bra and panties. She was something, I'll give you that much. Black hair all the way down her black. Blue eyes that filled up her face. She looked young, really young, but not under-aged or anything. Her body was unnaturally perfect, like it had been filled up with air in all the right places. Big, but nothing was sagging. She wasn't athletic, lithe or lean; it was more like she was spare, like there were parts of her that just weren't there.

When she danced, it was without any enthusiasm. Still, she didn't seem to be sulking so much as lazy. Just showing off the goods at a leisurely pace, like she knew that was all she had to do, and wasn't going to do anything else. Just spin back and forth in front of the mirror, tracing her hands all over the body, staring off somewhere with a composed, vacant look on her face.

She didn't look like the other Tanya, the one from before, and I felt a sensation of relief wash through me. That surprised me; I hadn't realized I was how worried about Dean until that moment. I looked at him to smile, to make some joke, and when I saw him all that tension clamped back down on my shoulders.

It wasn't that his eyes were bugging out of his head or anything like that. If you didn't know Dean, like I knew him, you might not have realized anything was wrong. There was very little expression on his face at all. It was how still he was. You couldn't even see him breathing. Hand in front of his mouth, elbow propped on the table, eyes forward. As if all his attention was covering onto a single point.

Shit, shit shit, I thought.

I turned my attention back to Chantelle and we talked back and forth for the next three songs. I kept asking her questions she wouldn't answer and she would laugh, and I kept saying: "No, but seriously. Seriously."

"Give it up for Tanya, that was Tanya gentlemen! She'll be available for private dances in just a few minutes."

Dean didn't wait. He just stood up and walked over to the bar, right where she would be coming out. The man with the cornrows started at him. Dean didn't notice. He was dialed in.

"Wow," Chantelle said. "Looks like your friend really took a shine to her."

"He's a romantic at heart," I said. "In fact, he's just coming out of a very bad relationship. Sensitive guy."

"Oh really," Chantelle said. "Because he's wearing a wedding ring."

"It's a tragic, tragic story," I said, shaking my head. "We lost a lot of good men out there."

"He married a man?

"You know what I mean," I said.

A moment later Tanya came out of the back and Dean walked up to her. She looked at him briefly for a moment, seemed to incline her head in a yeah, whatever gesture of distant assent, but then her eyes opened wider with fear and I knew that Dean had dropped Brucie's name.

Dean was talking to Tanya, opening up a notebook.

The guy with the cornrows came over.

Tanya was backing away.

"Can we go back for a dance?" I asked.

"Sure!" Chantelle said, and we stood up and headed to the back of the room. Behind me I heard Dean cry out. I took one glance over my shoulder, making sure they weren't killing him or anything. Dean was shouting "I'll go, I'll go!" and they didn't seem too rough. The dude with cornrows was staring at me, but not coming over.

"Uh oh," Chantelle said. "Looks like your friend got a little too romantic."

We went to the back room, and she laid on me, rubbing her back on my chest, for twenty bucks every three minutes.

"What's the deal with that girl?" I asked.

"Oh, her," Chantelle said. "She's Russian or something and she works for this shady escort agency. That guy, Desean, is like her bodyguard. He speaks Russian to her."

"Really?" I said.

"Yeah, he's a total gangster. Your buddy is lucky he didn't get the shit kicked out of him."

She turned around and put her tits in my face and showered me with her sweet-smelling hair.

"I don't even know why she comes here. I think it's just advertising for the escort business. She's super expensive."

"How do you know?" I asked. "Did you ever hire her?"

"Oh yeah," she said. "Every Saturday night."

She turned around again and made these fake moaning noises. I was getting hard anyway.

"So she runs around with a lot of rich guys?" I asked.

"Hockey players," she said.

"No way," I said.

"Oh yeah," she said.

"Like who? " I asked.

"Mikhail Novosi," she said.

I laughed.

"How do you know? Did she tell you?"

"No, his sleazeball agent is always in here, trying to get girls for parties. He's Russian too."

The music changed.

"Want another dance?" she asked.

"Got any more stories about crazy Russian call girls?"

"Fresh out," she said.

"Well then I'm good." I said.

I paid her and then I left. Desean stared at me as I made my way to the stairs. I found Dean waiting a little down the street.

"Thanks for the help in there buddy," Dean said. "Where the fuck were you?"

"Getting a lap dance," I said. "But don't worry. I figured out who the murderer is."

"Who?" he asked.

"Mikhail Novosi."

15

The next morning I felt down. It was about the stripper, Chantelle. I couldn't help but feel that back in the day, I'd have closed that deal. It wasn't just that I was fat. I'd never been much of a looker, but I would have just kept at it. I just didn't seem to want it as much anymore. I felt old, basically. Too old for the way that I used to do things, but I didn't know any other way.

Mr. Burke left home around 11:30 and went to Lucien for lunch with two fairly attractive women. I got some pictures but when it seemed clear that it was a business meeting, I went to Hero Burger for lunch and blew my diet.

While I was eating, my Blackberry rang. It was Dean.
"Hey buddy," he said. "How are you feeling this morning?"
"Old," I said.
"Peter from Paradise Comics e-mailed me. I forwarded it to you. Did you see that?"
"I've been working on another case," I said.
"The comic Brucie bought was originally submitted at some place called Over the Boards Collectibles in Mississauga. It mostly sells sports collectibles by the looks of things. Can you check out its website?"
"Okay," I said. "But I got work to do too you know."
"Hey man," Dean said. "You're the one that gets to bill for this. Besides, things are a little nuts here right now. The whole firm is tense because of Jay's situation with the OSC. Things will be better once that blows over."
"I was meaning to ask you about that," I said.

"It's just bullshit," Dean said. "It will go away. Also, I'm going to text you the details for Tanya's escort service. I got them from Rob's buddy. See if you can't set something up with Tanya."
"Now that's my kind of disbursement," I said.
"I can't do it myself because I blew it last night," Dean said. "I don't know what I was thinking."

For a beat I didn't answer, then I just said: "Yeah," and took a bite of onion ring.

"Apparently there's a little password and you have to say who referred you. It will all be in the text. See what you can do and we'll figure out what she knows. She knew who Brucie was, that's for sure."

I sucked the last of my coke through the straw and rattled the ice cubes around in the paper cup. Then I headed back to the office, booted up the computer, and went to overtheboards.com.

The store sold game-worn jerseys and other memorabilia, but mostly the website was dedicated to new and vintage sports cards with a big emphasis on hockey. I noticed, with interest, that the some of the trading cards had been authenticated by a company called Professional Sports Authentication and came in little plastic containers. A few minutes of online research revealed that PSA was affiliated with CQC.

Now, being from the South, I don't much give a shit about hockey, although I went to some Kings games in LA. But some of the hockey cards were pretty cool. I especially liked the 'Vintage Game Used Memorabilia Cards'. They'd have a picture of Alex Ovechkin, or whoever, and then a little tiny square of fabric from a jersey he'd worn. Or a very thin slice of a hockey stick he'd used. They were glossy and cool looking. I would definitely buy basketball cards like that.

Eventually I found the blog of the proprietor, a dude named Derek Ha. Mr. Ha, whoever he was, was seriously into hockey. There was a post every couple of days talking about the cards he was doing, when things were getting signed, new players he'd added, stuff like that.

One of the posts mentioned something like: "back when I had my problems with the CRA." That kind of piqued my interest, so I started skipping back by year. It looked like in the year of the NHL lockout (2003-2004) Over The Boards had a pretty tough year, financially.

I re-checked Brucie's account statements but I didn't see anything at a comic store after the $9,000 charge. Even so, I spent the afternoon looking up comic stores in Toronto online and calling them if they had a CQC account. None of the clerks I spoke to remembered Brucie, but they all promised to ask the other clerks about it.

Finally I called my buddy Milo and got him to set up the date with Tanya. Milo is well-to-do. He's a blue-collar Hungarian who runs a bunch of hot dog stands in the city. Nice guy, but not a looker, and no stranger to the ladies of the night. He called me back after the arrangements were made.

"It's all set," he said. "It better be worth it because it's going to cost me a thousand bucks."

"That's it?" I said.

"What do you mean that's it? That's a lot."

"I thought it was two."

"Two? That's fucking nuts. Who would actually pay that?"

"So when's the date?"

"Not till Saturday. She's coming over to my place."

"Great. Dean and I will be there."

"This better not be trouble," Milo said. "Last thing I need is a black guy getting knifed by a pimp in my apartment. Think of the property values."

"There goes the neighborhood," I agreed.

16

The next day Dean was jammed up at work, so I was alone when I strolled into Over The Boards Collectibles. Big place, huge. Racks and racks of colourful jerseys, signed photographs and posters on the walls, and glass cases filled with memorabilia.

Mr. Derek Ha was behind the counter, and he was a character. Asian, late forties, very short, with jet black hair parted very severely on the left side. He wore large glasses and he had braces. The store was pretty busy and he was talking to a couple of kids about some signed photographs of Alexander Ovechkin.

"Hello hello," he said. "How can I help you?"

"Hi," I said. "My name's Terrell Delacroix. I'm here about a comic book."

"We don't sell comic books," Derek said. "Try Altered States on Lakeshore."

"I'm not here to buy comics," I explained. "I'm here to talk about a comic that was submitted to CQC through your store a few years ago."

"Oh?" Derek said. "How do you know it was submitted here? I didn't know that CQC released that information to the public."

"Well, I got it anyway," I said.

"How did you get it?"

"Well, we made inquiries of CQC and they answered us."

"I think that information is private."

"Well," I said, "like I said, they gave it to us."

"I don't think I'm prepared to discuss this at all."

"But why?" I said. "You don't even know what I'm here about."

"I don't think I'm required," Mr. Ha said, his voice rising (which was a bit ridiculous, because he had a very high pitched voice) "to answer questions about information that was supposed to be held confidential."

"Mr. Ha," I said. "Let me explain to you what I'm here about. A young man killed himself. One of the last things he did was purchase a copy of Detective Comics #66 for $9,000. We just want to know if you can shed any light on that comic, whether you can remember anything about it in particular."

"No," he said. "I don't remember. I submitted hundreds of comics to CQC, even though I only did comics for two years. It was during the lockout. Sales of hockey cards were way down. I was already a member of PSA and I thought it was a good way to broaden my business a little."

"But it didn't work out?" I asked.

"I just didn't know what I was doing," he said. "It was nothing but headaches. People submit a comic and it doesn't come back with the score they want and who do they blame? Me. God forbid if it comes back restored. Those restorations are hard to spot and they take the value down to nothing. I had one guy threatening to sue me, saying I stole his comic. I stole his comic!"

Derek shook his head and continued.

"There's one thing you should know about me, Mr. Delacroix. My whole business depends on integrity. When I sell a signed picture, how does my customer know the signature is real? How do they know I didn't just sign it myself? They don't. They can't tell. They rely on my integrity. When I sell a game-worn jersey, how do they know the jersey was really worn in the game? My integrity. When I put a slice of a hockey puck in one of my signature series hockey cards, how do they know that's real? My integrity."

"Integrity is pretty important in a lot of businesses," I said. "A lot of people don't know exactly what they're buying and have to trust the store."

"Exactly," Derek agreed. "That's what that guy who said I stole his comic didn't understand. Could a jeweler sell a cubic zirconium to one of their clients and call it a diamond? Sure, most people can't tell the difference. But are they really going to jeopardize a whole business, a whole successful business, trying to rip off one guy?"

Derek smiled, and added: "That's why comics were so unpleasant for me. Plus, I don't even like comics! I just don't get the appeal. I prefer real-world heroes."

"Well, all right," I said. "You don't have any written records of who submitted this particular comic? I have the CQC number."

"I threw all that paperwork out," Derek said. "I don't remember. Can I help you with anything else?"

I shook my head. Mr. Ha went back to the computer behind the counter, and I left.

17

I spent Friday morning driving around the city after Anthony Burke, to no avail. A little before lunch on Friday my phone rang. It was a number I didn't recognize.

"Hey man, is this Terrell Delacroix?"

"It surely is. To whom am I speaking?"

"I saw your posting on Brucie's wall."

"On his what?"

"On Facebook."

"Right. Who are you?"

"My name is Jamie Halfin. Can I talk to you?"

"You're talking to me now."

"I mean, like, in person."

"What's this about?"

"Well, I was with Brucie a couple of days before he died, and it was a bit weird. I haven't told anyone about it. I feel like I should say something."

"You don't want to talk on the phone?"

"Nah man. Can you come up to Lawrence and the Allan? The Coffee Time just east of the Allan? I'm here now."

"Okay mystery man. You better be there though."

"I'll be there."

And he was, sitting at a booth in the far corner where he could see everyone coming in and out. A shifty little guy, thick glasses, curly hair, twisting a plastic straw into knots. His shirt didn't fit him; his neck was rattling around in his collar.

I ordered a doughnut, and it was dried out and crappy. Coffee Time sucks. I mean really. Who is so poor that they can't afford Tim Hortons? Who's like, "oh no man, Tim Hortons is too rich for my blood! I want to go to the budget version of Tim Hortons!"

I sat down in front of Jamie and eyed him skeptically.

"So what have you got to say?"

Jamie glanced around and then spoke.

"Look, Brucie and I were never close friends."

"Okay."

"But we went to the same private school. Upper Canada College? Anyway, I was kind of the school drug dealer. One day last year the cops were inside with one of those drug-sniffing dogs. I was fucked, hiding in an empty closet. Brucie saw me in there and took my stuff and flushed it for me. Real classy move, I thought. Like I said, he didn't even know me, and he was a popular kid."

"I thought Brucie was a dork."

"Yeah, but he was a cool dork," Jamie said.

I shook my head.

"You kids have such complicated lives. Back in my day, no one bothered to make different categories of dorks."

"Anyway," Jamie continued, "I told Brucie I owed him one. I didn't really think much about it. But he called me in late August to call in the favour."

"When?" I said, taking out my notepad.

"August 18. The Thursday. He said he needed my help the very next day. The idea was he would take my car and I would take his. I would wait for him in the underground parking lot of this hotel out near the airport. Then he would drive in with my car, we'd switch, and go our separate ways."

"What kind of car have you got?"

"A Honda. It's nothing special."

"And so did you do it?"

"Yeah, of course. It was weird, but I figured I owed him at least that much."

"So you waited in the parking lot ..."

"And he came in, driving really fast, and parked next to me. Then he popped out and got this black box out of the trunk."

"Whoa," I said. "A black box?"

"Yeah."

"What did it look like?"

"I don't know," he said. "It looked like it was made of plastic. I didn't get a good look at it. He just stuck it in the trunk of his car, we switched keys, and he drove out."

"And that was that?"

"Yeah," Jamie said. "And then a week later he's dead."

I carefully wrote everything down.

"How come you didn't tell the cops?"

"Well," Jamie said. "No one ever asked me about it. Like I said, we weren't really friends. And I was nervous about it. Like, what if I did something illegal?"

"Do you have any idea what was in the box?" I asked. "Was it heavy?"

"I don't know," Jamie said. "Not too heavy, I guess."

"All right," I said. "Thanks very much for the information."

"Will you tell the cops now?" he said.

"Maybe, eventually," I said.

"Well, let me know if you do. I didn't know I was doing anything wrong."

"You're pretty nervous about this for a drug dealer," I said.

"Yeah, you should definitely leave that part out," Jamie said.

"No problem, Mr. Halfin," I said. "I got your back."

He nodded.

"I feel terrible," he said. "Brucie was a good dude. He stone-cold carried three ounces of pot all the way to the washroom. He knew no one would search him, but what if the dogs sniffed it? They were yapping and pissing over everything. He didn't have to do that. He was a good dude. Whatever happened, it sucks."

"That's for sure," I said.

18

I didn't get up to much Friday night, which meant I woke up early Saturday morning. That kind of sucked, because if you're single, Saturday morning is one of the loneliest times. I tried to go for a run up Mount Pleasant to Sherwood Park. Within ten minutes I had to walk, wheezing, a dark stain spreading across the back of my shirt. I stayed out for almost an hour, anyway, then went back to my apartment and had some orange juice and watched the British Premier League soccer game on Sportsnet.

Let me tell you a secret: soccer is boring. I managed to sit through the first game, a 1-1 draw between Newcastle and someplace called "Everton", and that was all I could take. I had to do something else. I sent some texts out but I didn't even get a nibble. I checked my Facebook, nothing. So I broke down and called Dean's house. I thought maybe I could just go over there and hang out until our appointment. Maybe I could help with some gardening or something.

Tina picked up the phone.
"Terrell!" she said. "So nice to hear from you!"
"Hi Tina," I said. "How are you?"
"I'm good," she said. "I just got the baby to go to sleep."
"Great," I said. "I hope I didn't wake him up."
"Oh no," she said. "I set the phone to mute before I even start to try."
"Phew," I said. "What about Krystal?"
"Oh, she's out with her friends today," Tina said. "I worry about her. Dean says I worry too much. I just don't want her to make the same mistakes I did."
"Well," I said, "you turned out all right."
"That's what Dean says!" Tina said. "And of course he's right. We all have very nice lives. Still, I have a lot of regrets. Don't you?"

I opened my mouth to say, sure, of course, but whatever, or words to that effect. To my complete surprise there was a hard, painful lump in my throat, followed by a pricking feeling in my eyes. I said something like: "Ahhh." Then I was scared to try to say anything else.

Holy shit, I thought. *Am I going to fucking cry?*

"Terrell?" she said.

"Yeah," I managed. "Yeah, there's stuff I regret."

Like I said at the beginning of this book, I'm not one for flashbacks or dwelling on the past. So if you're hoping for a bunch of salacious details about California, you're out of luck. But maybe now's the time to mention that working in the porn industry can cast a shadow over your life. It's not that having sex on camera is actually any worse than what most other people do to pay the rent. It's the way people treat you, the stigma. Perception, opinion, can be such a real thing, such weighty, hefty thing. It's tougher to carry it than you think, especially when you get older and you slow down and tire out. When you're young it doesn't seem like a big deal. Fuck what other people think, right? But it does matter. Sure it does.

"But you're doing so well!" Tina said, her voice warm and generous. "You've got a great job and it sounds like you're doing really well."

"Yeah," I said, "things are good."

"Well you tell me if you start feeling sad, all right?"

"All right," I said.

"Do you remember Jacey?"

"No," I said.

"Sure you do," Tina said. "She was into all that jungle music, she had it on her computer?'

"Um," I said.

"She had the tattoo of a compass on her, on her back."

"Right," I said. "How's she doing?"

"She killed herself," Tina said.

"Fuck," I said.

"Yeah," Tina said. "I guess she was bulimic for a long time. They thought she was getting better."

"Who told you?"

"Rodney. We're friends on Facebook. Anyway, I guess she wrote her suicide note to her bird. Isn't that sad? She was going to kill herself, and the only person she thought would care was her bird."

The rate of substance abuse, depression and suicide for porn actors is rather high. When I worked in the industry there was this campaign to set up a hotline set up that adult performers could call in to get free counseling. It was called PAW (Protecting Adult Welfare). I remember a fundraising event they had that involved paying to watch porn actresses bowling in the nude. I think it raised under five thousand bucks. This in a five-billion-dollar industry.

"Yeah," I said. "Well, Tina, it was a good time, we had some laughs, we made some cash, and now we're home free."

"I hope so," Tina said. "Things were pretty tough down in California towards the end. I guess Dean told you about it?"

"Uh, sort of."

"Well, we had to do something. Dean was in rough shape. We just weren't getting along so well. Then I got pregnant and this opportunity came up and we thought maybe things would be different up here. But this new firm! Terrell, it's not healthy. They all work to ten pm every night. That's an easy-going night for them. And I don't know about this detective thing. It didn't work out with Tanya, remember? You guys couldn't prove anything and then Dean went back on drugs."

"Yeah," I said.

"I mean, what good ever came of it?"

"That was different though," I said. I felt like I was trying to convince myself. "You know Dean felt responsible for Tanya."

"But it was so long ago," Tina said. "It took him so long to get over it."

Here's the thing about Dean that I didn't say to Tina, but maybe I should have. Dean can get really emotional about stuff without showing it. For instance, when the shit went down right at the end of the Tanya thing, I lost it. Dean had to drag me off the guy or I'd have choked him to death (remember, I was still in shape back then). Just the look in that bastard's eyes, that fucking sly look. But two days later I was over it. Six months later I'd forgotten it. But Dean? He was as cool as a cucumber at the time, but now it was eight years later and he was still feeling it. That was the difference between him and me.

"He'll be okay," I said. "You know what he's like. But look at what his boss is going through. It's no wonder he feels like he has to help out. It's not like it was in California."

"Yeah," Tina said. "You're right."

"Is Dean around?"

"No," Tina laughed. "Of course not. He's at work."

"Well, talk to you later I guess."

"You know," Tina said, "you can come over any time. He doesn't need to be here for us to hang out."

And it would easy for me to play dumb here. Easy for me to say, oh, it just happened by accident, or we just fell into it. But I'm not going to bullshit you. I've probably slept with close to 200 women in my life. Yeah, I was in porn, but that only accounts for like thirty or so. I was a relentless force of nature, man. I was driven by wild desire and I was charming as hell. I know women. I can feel opportunities with them. And all that old machinery inside me, that had been unused for a while, started to hum.

"Yeah sure," I said, although I was resolved to go nowhere near her now. "Anytime."

Here is what I ended up doing: I went down to the grocery store and bought a bag of those little individually wrapped Babel cheeses. The ones that come in bright red wax. Then I unwrapped them, dipped them in egg, rolled them in bread crumbs, and put them in the deep fryer. After the first two I realized what they needed – hot sauce. I got halfway through the package and I knew I should stop but I was in the grip of some weird compulsion, like I couldn't relax until they were all gone. When it didn't make me sick I was more disturbed than relieved. Thankfully Spike TV was having a Star Wars marathon and I was able to pass most of the rest of the afternoon without thinking.

19

Milo lived in a nice condo in Liberty Village. The building was about five stories, with polite East Asian doormen and a garden on the roof. Milo had great parties there, many of them attended by me, and some of them almost getting him evicted, or whatever the equivalent of evicted is when you own the place.

Dean and I drove over together. Neither of us knew what to make of Jamie's black box story. Dean irritatingly refused to join me in speculating.

Milo met us at the door to his apartment and I gave him a hug, and then he shook hands with Dean.

"A little detective work tonight boys?" Milo said.

"Yeah," Dean said. "Should be good!" He smiled, and he looked happy, but he also looked a little jazzed up.

"So I think what we'll do," Dean continued, "is that Terrell and I will hang out in the closet. After the dude leaves we'll come out and talk to her. Then we pay."

"You got the money?" Milo said.

"In cash," Dean replied.

We drew the curtains so no one could see inside, sat on one of Milo's soft leather couches, and watched the hockey game for a while. Milo and I drank Bud Light Lime while Dean had a tomato juice. Eventually the phone rang. Milo picked it up and said. "Just a minute." And then pressed nine on his phone.

"They're on their way up," Milo said. "Sounds like a black dude."

Dean stood up, a little too quickly, and went into Milo's bedroom. I followed him and started to close the door behind us but he said: "No, let's go in the closet.

"Oh man," I said. "Seriously?"

"Come on," he said, and beckoned to me.

I sighed and followed him into Milo's shallow walk-in closet. Dean flipped off the light but left the door open, just a crack.

"You smell a bit like cheese," Dean said.

"Fuck you," I replied.

We waited just a little while and then there was a knock on the door.

"Hey, how you doing," we heard Milo say.

"Hello sir," another male voice said. "Are you Mr. Nagy?"

"Yes I am."

"My name's Desean, Mr. Nagy," the new voice said. "I hope you don't mind, but it's something we do with all of Tanya's new clients. Just a quick look around. Won't take a minute."

"Be my guest."

We heard Desean soft footsteps as he padded around the apartment. He came right in the bedroom, even went over to the bathroom door and peaked inside. For a minute I was like, fuck, is he going to find us?

But he padded back out again and I heard him speak.

"Okay," Desean said. "Thanks for your cooperation sir. I'm going to ask you to pay in advance."

"Credit card okay?" Milo said.

"I'm just going to take your number down, sir," Desean said. "That's how we do it. If you want to party with Tanya again we'll just use the same number before she comes over. Can you sign here?"

Before Desean left he said something to Tanya, and sure enough, it was in Russian.

The door closed.

"Can I get you a drink?" Milo said.

"Please," Tanya said. She had an accent but her English was good.

I was ready to get up, but Dean caught my arm and shook his head for a moment.

"You have a very nice condo," she said. "How much does it cost?"

"It was two-fifty when I bought it," Milo said. "One about this size sold for three-hundred a month ago."

"Wow," she said. "Have you lived here long?"

"About seven years," Milo said. "Rum and Coke okay?"

"Sure," Tanya said. "Oh, wow, you have a drink dispenser."

At this word, Dean made a face and stood up. We walked into the living room. Milo's expression was guilty. The girl, who was wearing a shimmery, clingy dress that showed off everything she had without being too slutty, looked terrified.

"Relax," Dean said. "All we went to do is talk. We have some questions about Brucie Goldstein."

The terror that had flashed across Tanya's face retreated to her eyes. She shook her head and said, with a stronger Russian accent, "Ah, sorry, I don't understand."

"Nice try," Dean said, and motioned towards the drink dispenser (it held six bottles upside down, all next to each other, so that you could squeeze out a perfect shot every time without spilling a drop). "You know what a drink dispenser is? You can talk condo valuations? You can answer questions about Brucie Goldstein if you want to."

She looked down, and when she looked back up again a couple of tears were shining in her eyes.

"Please," she said. "I cannot talk with you."

Dean pulled over an arm chair and sat across from her. He folded one foot onto his knee and opened a package of cigarettes. Before he lit it he remembered himself and looked at Milo.

"Go ahead man," Milo said.

"Do you smoke?" Dean said to Tanya.

She shook her head.

"What's your real name?"

"Oksana," she said. Her hands were folded in her lap and she was looking down. Her chest was heaving up and down a bit. This girl was hot.

"Where are you from, Oksana?"

"Ukraine."

"How long have you been here?"

"One year," she said, "and six months."

"Okay," Dean said. "And about this Desean character."

"He works for my company," she said. "Please, you should not tell him that I spoke with you. He is a very dangerous man."

"Don't worry," Dean said. "So who does he work for?"

"I don't know," she said. "Russians I think. I know it was Russians who brought me here. We landed in Montreal. Then I was sold."

"Sold?" I said.

She looked at me briefly and then looked back down.

"How old are you?" Dean asked.

"Twenty," she said. "I paid to come here. It didn't seem like very much money. It was a trick. When I was taken away from my village the men treated me very, very badly."

"Where do you live?"

"In an apartment at Jane and Finch."

"Why don't you run away?"

"I am here illegally," she said.

"You could try to get refugee status."

She shook her head.

"You do not understand my village," she said. "It was a uranium mine thirty years ago. Now? It is like one of those movies at the end of the world. Eleven-year-old children drunk. All the babies born from drunk mothers. Garbage in the streets. Not enough food. Toronto is like paradise. I am a prisoner, I am even a whore, but Desean does not beat me. They put money for me in a bank account. He shows it to me online. In six years I can go to school, or buy a house. Find a husband. If I go back to the Ukraine, I will lose everything. I will be a prostitute, but for five dollars a day."

Oksana seemed to have regained her composure. She motioned over to Milo who brought her the rum and coke and she took a sip.

"All right," Dean said, "let's talk about Brucie."

"Brucie was a boy. What about him?"

"Did you know he was dead?" Dean asked.

Her eyes widened

"Dead?"

"Yes," Dean said. "The police are calling it suicide. He fell from a bridge."

Oksana started to cry again.

"No," she said. "It's not true."

"I'm sorry," Dean said. "We were hired by Brucie's father to find out what happened to him. We traced him to you."

"I see," Oksana said, and wiped her eyes. Her thin shoulders were heaving up and down. "I'm sorry. I thought he went to school. I thought he forgot about me. He was just a silly boy."

"Tell me how you met him," Dean said.

"We met at the Brass Rail in May," Oksana said. "I was dancing. He came up for a dance. I thought to myself: this is a boy. I almost called security to throw him out. But he was paying, and so I took him to the back and danced for him. He was a funny boy. He kept talking very quickly, saying he loved me. After five songs I said: okay, enough. And I sent him away. But another night he waited outside the bar and spoke with me. I gave him the information to get in touch with me. So I saw him through the summer."

"Right," Dean said.

"He kept saying he loved me," Oksana said, "that he would protect me. But I said to him: you are silly! You can't protect anyone. You are a boy. Then he asked me if I could see him for free, if we could go on a date. He ran out of money, I guess. And I laughed at him. He was such a silly boy. So he said he would find more money. That was the last I saw him."

"Did he say anything about comics?"

"No, never."

"Nothing?"

"No," Oksana said. "Did he like comics? I am not surprised. He would not tell me. He was always talking like such a big man."

"Where did you meet with him?"

"Usually the Howard Johnson in Yorkville. One time we went to his parents' house. I think he wanted to show me he was very rich."

"Brucie didn't owe you any money?" I asked. "Or your boss?"

She rolled her eyes.

"The people I work for would not loan money to a seventeen-year-old boy. He paid in advance."

"Okay," Dean said. "We're done for now. Thank you for speaking with us. I know Brucie's father would really appreciate it. Thank you Oksana."

"Please," Oksana said, "don't tell anyone I spoke with you."

"We won't." Dean said. And then he opened his wallet, took out a business card, and handed it to her. "You seem like you think you've got it all figured out, and maybe you do. But if you change your mind, and you need a lawyer, I can likely get you one."

She took the card and looked at it.

"You might not believe this," Dean said, "but I knew girls like you. Girls that, well. They were beautiful and the thought they were smart and they would cash in and they'd be laughing. It didn't always work out. If things start to go bad I hope you'll call me or someone and get out. You don't have to do this. Really. You don't."

She stood up.

"Everyone," she said, "in this country is a silly boy. I thought it was just Brucie, but it is everyone."

She walked over to the bathroom and closed the door behind her. A moment later we heard the shower hiss on.

Dean handed the cash over to Milo.

"Thanks bud," Dean said. "We'll head out. When the charge shows up on your credit card statement, can you send it to us?"

"No problem," Milo said. "Let me know anytime you need me to hire some hookers for you. That's kind of like my superpower."

Dean left. Milo and I ended up having a drink to celebrate. Oksana left without saying goodbye.

20

I woke up at home in my bed, hung over. When I stirred a little I bumped into someone next to me. Blond hair spilt across my pillow. It was a woman, late thirties, early forties. One of Milo's buddies. I couldn't remember the night before so well, it was hazy. But I guess I'd picked her up.

In the bathroom I leaned against the wall and pissed for a long time. I wondered how to get rid of the girl. The trick, I find, is to already be eating your breakfast when they get up. Then you can be like: no, sorry, I can't get brunch! I already ate. Although the real fucking trick is to go to their apartment, and not yours. Too late for that.

The sordid little strategies a hundred hook-ups teach you. One time, I had this talk with Dean about genius. I mentioned how Mozart was a genius because he wrote a symphony when he was three years old. Dean said something like, well yes, but his first symphony sucked. I was like, still, isn't it awesome he wrote it? He said, well, yes, but his dad pressured him into doing it. Mozart didn't really write any good music until he was twenty.

It turned out that Dean had read a book about the subject, and the book said that it takes 10,000 hours to be great at something. So Dean basically said, sure, Mozart was a genius, a child prodigy, but he still put his 10,000 hours in and worked for it just like the rest of us suckers.

And then Dean said a funny thing: he said that if you loved something, and you did it all the time, you'd get good at it. So basically, it's that love that makes you strong in the end. Even though you might not start out any better at something than anyone else, if you love it, you'll keep doing it until you're amazing.

It was like that with me and women. I remember trying to pick them up when I was a kid. I sucked at it. But I just felt a burning need to hit on ladies. I loved every girl I met, I mean, really loved them. I got into what they were interested in, I chased them around, I liked to meet their parents. Eventually I got good at it. And it *was* just practice.

Dean, I guess, is almost the reverse of that. He just didn't feel that pull to get in there. It was like he was looking for something perfect. And of course, that meant he never got any practice. So he couldn't get the rare girl that he did like.

But the thing is, though, I got tired of it. I could still keep picking up, but it was like a routine. This series of moves I'd go through every time. And they still fall for it, but when they do, it's like they're falling for a person that isn't really me anymore.

Say what you will, in my younger days, I really did love all women I chased around, even if it was six at once. It's hard to explain, but I did. But now? Thirty- three, fat, don't give a fuck? The fire is gone, but I keep doing it, like a machine, like a series of reflexes that just kick in without my brain getting involved.

It's not cool, I mean it. All these women just falling in love with who I am on the surface. They don't love me, they love a bunch of rehearsed lines, a little game.

Was Dean shallow too? Falling for Oksana because of how she looked? Just like Brucie had done before him?

It's hard not be cynical about love when you get good at it. It's hard not to see it for what it is: a bunch of people buying something without ever opening the box.

21

On Monday I had a fruit cup for breakfast with a cup of green tea and arrived at the Burke residence just in time to catch Anthony coming back from his morning jog. Today he drove straight down to the AGO, spent the morning in meetings, and then had lunch in the fancy restaurant at the ROM, right by the window, so I watch him from across the street while I ate a burrito from Burrito Banditos. Next he went to the gallery for a brief visit, and then he drove to see some clients in an enormous house in Woodbridge. All par for the fucking course.

I got a bleep on my Blackberry while I was sitting in my car waiting for Burke to emerge from the McMansion. It was an e-mail from Milo. The charge for the hooker showed up, but it wasn't what I'd expected. I called up Dean.

"Hey man," I said. "Check this out. The charge showed up on Milo's bill, but it's not like the other ones. It's only $1,000 and it's to some fishing store on Sheppard Avenue West."

"Really?" Dean said. "A fishing store?"

"Yeah," I said. "Weird."

"Well, I guess we should check that out too."

"I'll go now," I said.

"Aren't you going to get stuck in traffic?"

"No," I said. "I'm in Woodbridge."

"Nice," he said. "Woodbridge is lovely this time of year."

I put the phone away and got going.

Sheppard Avenue West struck me as an odd place for a fishing store. It was in a shabby little strip mall between a convenience store and a Turkish restaurant. A sandwich board advertising $40 psychic readings was further down the sidewalk. The bright yellow sign over the store read: SHEPPARD FISHING. A hand lettered note pinned to the front door read LIVE BAIT.

Really? I thought. *Live bait?*

The bell dingled as I went inside. The store, predictably, was empty. Fishing poles leaned up against the walls next to old posters for Ontario's provincial parks. A few life preservers dangled from hooks. Everything seemed to be coated with a fine layer of dust.

The man behind the counter looked a little like Paul Newman. Same short white hair, clear blue eyes, and unlined face. He was reading a copy of *Foreign Affairs* and watching me without much interest. He did not ask if I needed anything.

"It says here you've got live bait?" I asked.

The man nodded.

"Can I have some?" I asked.

"What kind?" he asked. He had a faint English accent.

"Uh, worms," I replied.

"What kind of worms?" he asked.

"I don't know man. I'm going up to Lake Muskoka today."

"On Monday?" he asked.

"Yeah, this way we beat traffic," I said. "Since I was driving by I just thought I should get some bait."

The man looked at me for a long time, and then he stood up and walked into the back room. I waited, feeling a bit like an idiot, for what seemed like a long time. But the man came back with a paper bag and handed it over to me.

"Five dollars," he said.

"Credit card okay?"

"Two dollar charge," he said.

"Fine by me."

While he was running it through, I asked:

"Do you fish yourself?"

"Yes," he said, "sometimes."

"I'm not much of a fisherman," I said.

"Hmm," he replied.

"Why do you like it?" I asked.

"Oh, it's relaxing."

"You don't find it boring?"

"Fishing requires patience," the man said. "It's important to be very patient."

I took my receipt and smiled at him.

"Have a good day," I said.

"Enjoy your trip," the man said.

Although he lifted his copy of *Foreign Affairs* back up, his eyes stayed on me until I left the store.

22

Tuesday morning I made some follow up calls to the comic stores to ask about Brucie, and this time I had better luck. The first guy I talked to at the first store I called (the Silver Snail on Queen West) knew exactly what I was talking about.

"Oh yeah," the guy said. "I remember him. Husky kid, right? Curly brown hair?"

"Yeah," I said. "That sounds like him. His name is Brucie Goldstein."

"Well, he said his name was Arthur Smith. But he didn't show any ID and he paid in cash."

"It was a Detective Comics #66? And he came in last July? Late in the month?"

"Sure, yeah, I remember," the guy said. "I remember because the comic came back 9.2."

"No shit?"

"Restored."

It took a moment for that to sink it.

"What?" I said.

"Needless to say I was a bit concerned what the kid would do when he found out. If it hadn't come back restored, that comic was worth up to 30 grand. Shit. Maybe more, what with Two-Face being in the last movie."

"He must have been pissed."

"You'd think," the guy said. "The funny thing is he didn't look that upset. He looked blank. Maybe he was in shock. Eight grand. Jesus."

"What do you mean eight grand?"

"Well, I asked the kid where he bought it. He said he bought it for eight grand in a private sale online. I told him he should call the cops, but I never saw him again."

"Thanks man," I said. I took down his name and contact info and then I hung up. Right away I called Dean.

"I think I figured out why Brucie killed himself," I said. "He tried to restore that comic."

23

Later that evening, around seven, we sat in Dean's backyard, sipping ice water with cucumber in it. Dean listened to everything I had to say about Derek Ha and my conversation with the guy at the Silver Snail.

"I know there's a lot of weird stuff about this case," I said. "The black box, the calls. But don't you think this just looks more and more like a suicide?"

"Think so?" Dean replied.

"Sure. Brucie starts seeing a hooker. He loves her. He's a bit unstable about it. Pretty soon he runs through all his money. So what does he do? He hatches a scheme to make some money. He'll take a comic book with a big spread on the grading notes, and resubmit it. But he's not going to just leave things to chance. He restores it a bit too. He was an artist, remember. Unfortunately, CQC catches him out. Faced with a huge pile of debt, he jumps off the bridge."

"Hmm," Dean said.

"What do you mean hmm? Just tell me what you're thinking, you fucker."

"Well," Dean said, "you're operating under the assumption that Brucie bought this particular comic because he looked at the grading notes and saw the scores were spread apart. But remember, he sent Paradise Comics a list. If he was looking for a comic with a big spread of grading notes, he could have just browsed through what they had in stock. Don't you think he must have had some other reason for sending the list?"

"But he asked to see the grading notes, and there's nothing on them other than the different scores and comments about the comic."

"Oh no?" Dean said.

He pulled out a copy of the grading notes from a manila folder and set it in front of me.

I looked over them.

"See? It's just about which corner is bent, or whatever ..." I began.

Dean's finger jabbed down at the top right corner of the page, where it was stamped with a date. February 18, 2004.

"The date?" I asked. And then I said: "Oh shit."

"The year of the NHL lockout," Dean said. "When our buddy Mr. Ha had a CQC account."

"Fuck," I said.

"Now we don't know what comics Brucie put on his list," Dean continued, "except for the two that were mentioned in the e-mail back to him. I did a little browsing on Heritage, the auction site that Peter mentioned. You can browse their history to see everything they've sold for years. Back in 2004 and 2005, Over The Boards sold over thirty comics, including both mentioned in Peter's e-mail to Brucie. Heritage's site even lists the CQC numbers."

"You think he bought this comic because he knew it was submitted at Over The Boards?" I asked. "But why?"

"Well," Dean admitted, "I don't know yet."

"I don't know Dean," I said. "It seems like a bit of a stretch."

"I just find it a weird coincidence," Dean said. "I don't know how else to explain the list."

"The list could be anything," I said. "He could have picked them based on how much their value changes by a point or two over 9.0."

"Could be," Dean said. "But here's what I'm thinking. Let's see if we can find the other comic on Brucie's list that was submitted through Over The Boards. Then we'll buy it and crack it open to have a look-see."

"Okay," I said. "We'll need the money to buy the comic though."

Dean waved his hand.

"We can always resubmit it afterwards anyway and resell it. We shouldn't lose too much money. Jay will pay."

"Up to you," I said, and had a drink of my cucumber water. "You're right that there's not much else to do."

"Actually," Dean said. "There is one other thing."

"What?"

"Well," Dean said, "you remember that Chantelle told you that Oksana parties with NHL players? Specifically Mikhail Novosi?"

"Yeah," I said.

"Well," Dean said. "Don't you think it's an interesting coincidence that the comic Brucie bought was submitted to CQC through a store that principally sells hockey memorabilia?"

I hadn't thought of that.

"I checked out Over The Board's website today," Dean said. "They have loads of stuff signed by Novosi. Cards, pictures, jerseys. They even had him in the store during the summer for an appearance. He was signing pictures and stuff. It was all on the blog."

"That is a weird coincidence," I said.

"So maybe you should look up what you can find on Novosi," Dean said. "I'd like to drop by and meet him sometime."

"And say what?" I asked. "Hey, I hear you like to party with hookers?"

Dean smiled.

"I'll think of something," he said.

Tina came out bearing a tray of snacks, and we dropped the subject for a while.

24

When I got to my computer the next morning I saw that Dean had e-mailed Peter (and cc'd me) about the comic he was looking to buy. Peter had already e-mailed back saying he didn't have it in stock but he could look around.

I also tracked down an address for Novosi. He lived in a condo in the big concrete forest at Lakeshore and Spadina. When I spoke to Dean about it, he said that the Leafs had a game Saturday night, so maybe we could catch him on Friday afternoon if we dropped by unannounced.

So for the better part of two and a half days, I followed Mr. Burke around the city. It was hard as hell to keep him in sight without making myself conspicuous. I didn't catch him doing jack.

Dean and I met up Friday at five pm. He came down from his office looking a bit raw. Red eyes, hair messed up, a few days worth of beard.

"You okay?" I said, a bit concerned.

"Oh yeah," Dean said. "Just working late on another file."

"Great," I said.

"I got an e-mail from Peter," Dean said. "Looks like the Hulk one he offered to Brucie is still available. The CQC number proves that it was submitted by Over The Boards and we can buy it for $6,000."

I whistled.

"We'll get the money back," Dean said. "I just want to take a look at it."

While we were heading west on King I stopped to buy a hotdog. For a while I'd resisted trying that weird corn jam that all the hotdog stands have in Toronto, but now I was getting addicted to it. I also went with bacon bits, mayonnaise, barbeque sauce and olives.

"Fuck man," Dean said. His tone was a mixture of disgust and awe.

"Don't knock it till you try it," I said.

"Duly noted," Dean replied.

I don't know why they put all the condo buildings in the city right next to each other. It makes for a depressing neighborhood; as sterile as an industrial zone, or Chernobyl. Fifty buildings stand together, right on the lake, nothing but concrete and empty roads between them. From the middle of them it's a 15 minute walk to the real city. I guess if you're lucky you get a nice view of the lake. If you're unlucky, you get a not-so-nice view of the condo building right next to you.

"How are we going to get in?" I asked Dean. "Buzz up?"

"Nah," Dean said. "Let's just try it the easy way."

So we hung around the front door until someone came out of the building and just walked in right after them. The guy leaving, a skinny Asian dude, even held the door open for us. Dean nodded at the doorman and we took the elevator up to the 36th floor.

"The simplest solution is best," Dean said.

Loud, pulsing techno music was coming from Mikhail's apartment. Dean knocked hard.

"What are you going to say?" I asked,

"Just follow my lead," Dean said.

There was no answer for a few seconds, so Dean pounded on the door again.

This time it opened, revealing a shirtless man, with a fat face, very short hair, and an evil expression in his eyes.

""Hey," Dean said, "I'm here to talk to Mikhail about a sponsorship."

The fat man lifted his eyebrows.

"Not here about music?" he said, with a Russian accent.

"No, no, I'm from TQ Sports. The jewelry company? I'm here about a sponsorship. We want to pay him to wear jewelry."

I didn't think it was going to work, but the fat guy stepped aside.

"Come in, come in!" he said. "Make yourself at home!"

So we walked in.

Great view, first of all. That was the first thing I noticed. Ceiling to floor view of the lake. Big balcony. A staircase curled up to a second floor. It was open concept, with a gleaming kitchen and a wide TV on the wall. White leather furniture. Nothing on the walls.

Two men, both in their underwear, were playing NHL 11 on the television. From where we were standing I could only see their hairy backs and their balding pates. A still-frosty bottle of Stolichnaya vodka was sitting on the table in front of them. The whole place smelt a little close.

"Come in, come in," the fat guy said. "Have a drink!"

"No, that's okay," Dean said. "Where's Mikhail?

"On the balcony," the fat guy said.

And there he was. I'd missed him the first time because he was off to the side. He was sitting out there in nothing but his shorts, gripping a hockey stick between his legs, and applying a blow torch to the blade. His face was lean, scarred with the ghost of teen acne, and carried an expression of almost fanatical focus. Every now and then he would press the blade into the railing of the balcony, look at it again, and test it on the ground.

"I'll just go talk to him," Dean said. "Terrell, wait here."

The two boys on the couch glanced at him as he crossed the room, and then went back to their game.

"You sure you don't want vodka?" the fat guy asked.

"No, I'm cool," I said. "I'll just wait for my buddy."

"Caviar?" the fat guy said. "Wine? Beer? Water? Pizza? We have left over pizza, I think. Sausage and garlic? From Amato?"

"No, no," I said. "I'm good."

"Please," the fat guy said. "You insult me."

He had to shout to be heard over the music. His breath stank of booze.

"Pizza," I said.

The guy grinned and got the box out of the fridge.

"Where's the bathroom?" I asked.

The guy motioned back the way I had come and I took my pizza there. When I glanced over my shoulder I saw Dean talking to Mikhail out on the balcony. Dean was showing him some sort of jewelry, looked like silver and gold chains, from a slim black carrying case. Mikhail was looking at the jewelry but still holding the blowtorch to the blade of his stick.

To my surprise, the bathroom was full of hockey memorabilia. Mostly sticks and jerseys, carelessly piled in the bathtub, but there were also stacks of cards and magazines on the counter next to the toilet, along with a big pad of what appeared to be clear stickers. A mug, bearing the Toronto Maple Leafs logo and full of sharpie markers, sat on the toilet tank. Finally, there was a plastic box of signed hockey cards next to the toilet. The cards were from all different brands and they all bore different pictures but the same player was on every one. Mikhail Novosi.

The sink and the tub were clean except for a fine layer of dust. No toothbrush, no shampoo, no soap. The cupboards under the sink and behind the mirrors were empty. It looked like the only thing that had ever been used was the toilet, like Mikhail only came in here to take dumps and sign memorabilia. Apparently at the same time. Delightful.

I took a whiz while eating my piece of pizza with my free hand. It was pretty thin so I folded it in half and I had finished it all before I was done peeing. Afterwards, I looked around for the hand soap but there was none to be found.

Instead, the garbage can caught my eye. It was tucked a little bit behind the toilet, and it appeared to be stuffed with brown wrapping paper and envelopes. Now, as you may or may not know, the courts have consistently ruled that there's no privacy interest in your garbage. So that means as a private detective a good portion of your day involves sorting through the trash. These are things they don't show you in Humphrey Bogart movies. Anyway, maybe it was just a reflex, but I pulled it out and start pawing through it. All of it was mail addressed to Novosi concerning the memorabilia he was signing.

I found a letter from Over The Boards.

Dear Mr. Novosi, we have not yet received the 300 cards we needed for the start of the season. As you recall, you were paid $3,000 for these signatures. It is important to us to get those cards in the packs so we can distribute them to our loyal collectors. I hope you have not misplaced the cards as they contain authentic game-used memorabilia and cannot be easily reproduced. I consider myself to have a good relationship with you and Vasily and I would *not want a minor matter like some signed cards to get in the way of that. Please contact me immediately if there are any issues. Yours truly, Derek Ha.*

I put the letter in my pocket and searched for anything else from Ha, but there was nothing. A quick search through the stack revealed the Over The Boards cards awaiting signature. Each one had a thin sliver of real wood attached to the front, and there was a hologram on the back. I thought about taking one but in the end I left them.

There was a thumping on the door.

"Just a minute," I said.

"I'm coming in," the voice said, and the door bumped open. One of the guys who had been playing video games staggered in, the music pouring in with him. "It's okay! Don't worry! I'll use the sink."

"Hey man!" I said. "Don't do that, it's cool!"

"No, no," the man said, and gestured at me to use the toilet. "It's all right! I don't mind! Go ahead, go ahead! Sink is fine."

He was already pissing. His urine was as clear as lake water, and stank like turpentine.

"What's the matter?" the man said. "Are you worried about sizes? I don't care about sizes, my friend. Go ahead."

I laughed at patted him on the back as I made my way outside. The fat guy who had let Dean and I in had taken a place at the television. They had switched to some game that involved shooting Nazis, and they were singing a song I recognized (from Rocky IV) as the national anthem of the Soviet Union. Their voices were barely audible over the techno, which had apparently been turned up.

Outside Dean was talking on an iPhone. It was not his and I assumed it belonged to Mikhail, who had returned to working on his hockey stick and was smoking a cigarette. Dean glanced at me, held up his hand, and said a few more words. Then he passed the phone back to Mikhail and made his way out to meet me.

"Let's go," he shouted.

We passed the sink-urinator in the hall; he gave us a little salute. Then finally we got out of the deafening condo into the hallway and summoned the elevator.

"How'd you come up with that jewelry line?" I asked Dean.

"It's a real company," he said. "One of my buddies' buddies is running it. "

"Did you get any info out of him?"

"As soon as he heard what I was there for he gave me his phone and told me to call his agent. Guy named Vasily Bogdanov. Mikhail said he didn't give a shit but he was getting in trouble for signing things without reading them."

"And so did you talk to him?"

"Yep. Sounds like a wheeler dealer. Apparently he's playing poker tonight some place on Spadina."

"There's a casino on Spadina?"

"Well, not a legal one," Dean said. "Do you know any way we could get in there? Vasily said we'd have to figure out our own way in."

"I might," I said, thinking of Mikey. "But what about the hookers? Did you ask about them?"

"I told him I'd heard he liked to party. He just sort of grunted. I didn't want to pry."

"So you didn't mention Brucie?"

"No," Dean said. "I just got the feeling I didn't want to tip our hand just yet. Let's talk to these guys a bit, get to know them."

"Well, whatever man. Anyway, look what I found."

I showed him the letter from Over The Boards.

"Holy shit," Dean said.

"Yeah."

"Well, that's quite a coincidence. These guys just happen to party with Brucie's hooker, and also have a business relationship with the store where he bought his comic."

"Agreed," I said. "It's weird."

"Well, good work. But remember one thing."

"What?"

"I'm Holmes. You're Watson."

"Fuck you, you racist."

"I'm not racist. There's nothing wrong with being Watson. You're a very good Watson."

"That's the soft bigotry of lowered expectations," I said.

Dean laughed as we stepped into the elevator.

25

By this time it was six. I called Mikey once we were outside. Sure enough, he knew about the poker game and he thought he could get us in. So we went our separate ways and then we reconvened at Dundas and Spadina a little after nine.

It was a big, plain looking building with few windows, more like a residential apartment building than a commercial unit. You could see the neon lights of Chinatown just to the north. Mikey was wearing a white shirt and denim overalls. An afro pick was stuck in his hair and he was sucking on a lolly pop. He looked like a whiter, sissier, version of Ice Cube from Boys N The Hood.

"Hello gentlemen," he said. "I hope you're ready for some poker. Do you have money?"

"Sure," Dean said.

"Great," Mikey said.

He dialed in the buzzer and after a moment a big black guy came down and opened the door.

"Hey Mikey," the bouncer said.

"Hey Marcel."

"Who are these guys?

"Friends of mine. Is there space at the tables?"

"Sure, it's still early."

Marcel held the door open for us and we jogged up three flights of stairs. When we got up top we had to wait, because the iron door was bolted shut. Marcel came up behind us, knocked, and it swung inwards. We went inside.

It was not a fancy place, I can tell you that much. Three or four tables were crammed inside, only one of which was occupied. The dealer was a big fat man, no neck, multiple chins, who looked at us very quickly with his little black eyes. Another big guy was standing next to the door, this one Russian-looking with very short blond hair and a tight t-shirt.

At the far side of the room an old lady with a cashbox was sitting behind a desk. Mikey went up to her and gave her 500 bucks, and she quickly but precisely counted out a stack of chips. I looked back to Dean for assistance (it didn't look like they took credit cards) but he was already producing a whack of cash.

"Be careful with it," he said.

We both got our chips. They opened up a new table for us. I sat down with Mikey, an Asian woman, and a smooth-faced bald dude wearing sunglasses indoors who looked like he might surprise his neighbours one day by turning out to be a serial killer. He kept smiling at me, like we were sharing some kind of joke.

Dean sat at the next table with Vasily and three other men.

A thick mullet lay on the back of Vasily's neck but the top of his head was bald. He had a handlebar moustache so nasty that most of the pornstars I'd known would have shaved it off. The suit he was wearing was as shiny and plastic-looking as the table cloth at the Chinese restaurants up the street, and his purple shirt was unbuttoned half-way down his chest. A gold cross glinted from the forest of his chest hair. A massive stack of chips sat in front of him, as well as a tall glass of vodka.

Our dealer sat down. He was an old man, really worn looking, with blue spidery tattoos on the back of his wrists.

"Let's play some cards," Mikey said.

So the cards scattered around the table. I folded every hand. After a few minutes the old woman gave me a glass of Vodka in a plastic cup with a picture of Ronald McDonald on it. I held it to my face but it smelt like gasoline, so I put it back down again.

At the other table, Vasily was winning. It was making him gregarious, and he kept chirping at the other people at the table in his heavy accent.

"I'm bluffing," he would say. "Come on, please. Call me. I'm begging you."

At our table, the serial killer smiled and nodded at me.

"He's in a good mood because he's winning," he said.

"Yeah, looks like" I said.

"He's the worst poker player ever," the serial killer said. "Too bad I'm not at his table anymore."

I looked at my hand. Jack Queen. Too risky. I folded.

"Yeah, too bad," I said.

"A month ago he was banned from here," the serial killer told me. "He owed them too much money. Like thirty grand."

"Just play cards," our dealer said, and gave the creepy dude a hard look. "Stick to the cards."

At the other table I could hear Dean talking to Vasily, telling him that he'd talked to him on the phone about the jewelry.

"You are a lawyer?" Vasily said. "Are you a Jew?"

Dean missed a beat, but then said, no, he wasn't a Jew.

"Too bad," Vasily said, with genuine regret. I mean, regret for Dean, like it was too bad for Dean that he wasn't Jewish. "Have you heard the joke about Rabinovich and the wolf?"

"It's on you," my dealer said, and I folded after giving my cards a token glance.

"So Rabinovich is walking with his sheep in a dark wood, and the two of them fall into a deep hole. They cannot get out. While they are down there a wolf falls in with them. The wolf sees the sheep, it begins to growl, to salivate." Vasily carefully pronounced this last word. "The sheep is afraid, it starts to cry out. And Rabinovich says, 'What do you mean, bah bah! Comrade Wolf knows who he is going to eat!'"

Vasily laughed at his own joke, and I heard Dean chuckle. To be honest I didn't really get it. At my table, Mikey was raising every hand. He had added a fair bit to his pile of chips but he did not look satisfied with it. That's the problem with gamblers. They're not really after money, they want to feel excited. I'm just scared of losing.

"Jewelry I don't know," Vasily was saying.

"We can set you up with a bunch of pretty nice stuff," Dean said. "The whole crew. He's just to make sure to wear it during press conferences, during interviews, around town."

"I have to inspect contract," Vasisily said. "I will give you my BBM. Pass me your card."

Dean handed it over.

"Also," Dean said, "let me know if you have any spare hockey tickets. People at the office are always looking for them."

"Yeah?" Vasily said. "Lots of rich lawyers at your firm?"

"Sure," Dean said. "Two hundred, and the poorest one makes one-thirty a year."

Vasily grunted.

"Good to know," he said.

"You've got to play if you want to sit at the table," my dealer said to me. "Not this hand, of course, but. You know. Soon."

"Dude," I said, "I feel you, but you're dealing me shitty cards here. These are some very shitty cards."

"Sometimes you do not get the cards you would like," the dealer said. "You still have to play your hand. Unless God wills it, no one is a winner."

The next hand I got the 6 and 7 of hearts. Mikey raised me like a goof and I called. There were two hearts in the flop, and so I hung around even though Mikey raised me before the turn and the river. No more hearts though. I tried to bluff Mikey at the end, but he called me.

"Well, you got me," I said, putting down my cards. "This is why I don't gamble."

"Jesus Christ," Mikey said, disgusted.

He threw down his hand, pocket jacks.

"I know, I suck."

"You suck all right," Mikey said. "But you have a straight."

The dealer was pushing the chips towards me, grinning. One of his front teeth was gold.

"Women's jewelry, no," Vasily was telling Dean at his table.

"Really?" Dean said. "No special ladies in your life? No one at all? I heard you like to party."

"Is that so?" Vasily said. "Well, I don't give presents to any woman except my mother. Women are either ugly, in which case, no jewelry will help, or they are beautiful, in which case, jewelry is just coals to Newcastle." Again he pronounced the English expression very carefully. "Do I party? Yes. But I party like a man, Dean. Perhaps one day you will see."

"Oh," Dean said, "I'm a married man. I don't think that's in the cards."

A little more time passed, and then I heard Dean getting up behind me.

"Well, that's that," Dean said.

"Keep playing my friend," Vasily said. "Soon your luck will change!"

"Nah," Dean said. "I gotta get home."

Dean left quickly. Mikey was reluctant to go, he was just getting into it, but eventually we cashed out and jogged down the stairs. Dean was waiting for us. He had lost his whole five hundred, mostly to Vasily.

"So do you really suck at poker?" Mikey asked. "Or is it all part of your scheme?"

"Can't it be both?" Dean asked.

"He's like Homer Simpson," I said. "He sucks like a fox."

"Well, now what?" Mikey asked. "Are you guys going out? Otherwise I'll just end up going home and losing this on Party Poker."

"I gotta get back home," Dean said.

"Going to see the wife?" I said, making an obscene gesture with my hips.

"No, she's asleep."

"Well, then you've got time for some Chinese food," I said. "Let's go to Lucky Seven."

Lucky Seven was one of those restaurants that don't really get going till around 4 in the morning, when the bars empty out. It was nice to be there when it wasn't full of drunks. The white walls were covered with gold and red posters of dragons, and the tables sported shiny disposable plastic tablecloths that can get ripped away with a flick of the wrist.

"Man," I said. "I don't think I've ever been here sober and before midnight before."

Mikey and I ordered while Dean fiddled with his Blackberry.

"How's Tina doing?" I asked.

"Good," Dean said, as the waiter came back and set down a small white pot filled with weak tea. "She's not happy about how much I work. But it's not going to be like this forever."

"Right," I said.

It was impossible to pour the tea without spilling it, so the pale yellowish liquid pooled on the plastic table cover.

The food came. We got one of those big pots of hot soup with all the little chili peppers floating in it, topped with a shimmering layer of oil. Snow peas, General Tao Chicken, spicy eggplant, and rice.

Over dinner, Mikey asked Dean:

"So what do you think about Goldstein getting added to the notice of allegations?"

"Jay is my mentor," Dean said, "and I think that it's bullshit."

"Aw man, I'm sorry," Mikey said. "For what it's worth I think they're stretching too. It's all just a lot of Monday morning quarterbacking."

"It's not even that," Dean said. "He said what the fucking law was. A board member's personal opinion of the share price isn't a material fact."

"What's up with Jay?" I asked.

"Well," Dean said, "the OSC decided, after its investigation, to bring him into their court case against Edenfree."

"Is he going to go to jail?" I asked.

"No, no," Mikey said. "He might get fined, that's all. The real issue is, what's the law society going to do?"

"Nothing in the short term," Dean said. "But if he's found to have acted against the public interest, that could change. It will be years before it goes to a hearing."

"What does he do in the meantime?"

Dean shrugged.

"Jesus," Mikey said. "What a shit show. It's a funny profession we've chosen."

"Dean," I said. "Does this affect anything we're doing?"

"Not unless he says so," Dean said. "Just keep at it. Maybe we'll solve the case. Cheer him up a bit."

Dean paid for dinner and left. After considering a number of bars, and texting a lot of people, and being unable to come up with something satisfactory, Mikey and I headed our separate ways. I fell asleep early.

26

I was faced with another Saturday morning where I wasn't hung over and didn't have much to do. So I got out my laptop and went to the webpage of the Ontario Securities Commission.

It was pretty easy to find the Amended Notice of Allegations because it was the first thing on the first page. I clicked on it and a pdf opened up. The word <u>Amended</u> was underlined in the title, and so was the name "Jason Goldstein" in the list of the respondents. I guess all of the parts that had been added recently were underlined like that, and so it was pretty easy for me to track down the paragraphs that had to do with Jay.

Before releasing the prospectus, Nolan consulted with Jason Goldstein, an Ontario lawyer. Goldstein advised the Board that they did not need to disclose his concerns about the long-term stability of Edenfree.

By providing that advice to Nolan, Goldstein acted contrary to the public interest.

To me, that sounded brutal. I really had trouble understanding how it could be no big deal, as Dean kept saying. I made a mental note to ask him about it.

I met Dean at Paradise Comics just a little after lunch and we went in together.

"Thanks for your help," Dean said to Peter.

"Like I said," Peter said. "Anything for Jay."

Peter handed Dean the box and Dean looked at the comic inside. The Hulk, wearing nothing but his conveniently indestructible purple pants, was battling Wolverine, who was springing forward with his claws pointed at the reader. It was graded 9.6.

"The first appearance of the greatest Canadian super hero," Peter said. "It's all to your liking?"

"Guess we'll find out," Dean said, and then he took out his keys and popped the box open.

"Fuck," Peter said. "You still have to pay for that."

Dean took the comic out of the box.

"Can you take a look at this for me?" Dean said. "Let me know if you see anything unusual?"

"Dude, I told you," Peter said. "That's what CQC is for. They graded it 9.6."

"Humour me," Dean said.

Peter sighed. I wondered whether he was going to put gloves on, or use tweezers, or anything like that, but he just carefully handed the comic around the edges, gingerly turning the pages and glancing at each one. Slowly, a frown appeared on his face.

"What?" Dean said.

"Something seems … off about it."

"What? It's not real? It's restored."

"No," Peter said. "I mean, no. I don't know."

"You don't know?"

"It looks fine," Peter explained. "I can't say for sure anything is wrong. It just feels sort of off. The colours in some of the panels. And the edges of the paper."

Peter took out a ruler from under the counter and measured the dimensions of the comic.

"I don't know," he said again.

"Would you still pay six grand for it?" Dean asked.

"Dude, you have to buy this comic," Peter said.

"I know, but I'm just asking."

Peter held the comic for a long time.

"Not six grand," he said finally. "I'd pay three. I mean it looks good. And this is another book where a few points make a big difference. A 9.9 sold for $150,000, I believe."

"Can you resubmit it to CQC for me?" Dean said.

"No man, you have to buy it!" Peter said.

Dean laughed.

"Yeah, yeah, after I buy it. Then I'd like you to resubmit it for me, on a rush basis if possible."

"Time shouldn't be too much of a problem," Peter said. "This is a valuable comic and they aren't going to sit on it for long."

"Great," Dean said, and took out his credit card. It was a Minnesota Timberwolves MBNA Mastercard. You would never know the dude made six figures.

Peter visibly relaxed once the transaction cleared.

"You know if this doesn't come back your way you don't get your money back," Peter said.

"Yep," Dean replied. "That's how the game is played."

And at this he gave me a wry look and smiled.

"You pay your money," he said, "and you take your chances."

27

Dean asked me if I'd had lunch and I lied and said no. We walked across the street to Gabby's and ordered a pitcher of coke and two pounds of hot wings. The weather was a bit grey and grizzly, but we sat right next to the open window anyway. Dean doesn't mind the cold, he never has. It drives me nuts but I just left my jacket on, even though we were inside.

"How's Jay doing?" I asked.

"He seems okay," Dean replied.

"Dean," I said. "I gotta say I don't get it. You keep saying it's no big deal, but it seems like a big deal to me."

"I know it does," Dean said, "but it's not."

"How could it not be a big deal for him to tell the board they don't have to tell the shareholders the company is overvalued?"

"Jesus," Dean said. "So Edenfree was a private bank and they sold asset-backed commercial paper, or ABCP. Do you know what that is?"

"Bundles of mortgages?"

"It could be mortgages, yes, but it could be all sorts of things. It could be credit card debt, or auto loans, or student loans, or I don't know what. Now do you know what an IPO is? An initial public offering?"

"Yes."

"Really?"

"No," I confessed.

"There are two kinds of companies, public and private. The difference is that for public companies, you can buy and sell its shares on the stock market. And those companies have certain disclosure obligations. They need to tell everyone how much money they're making and how their business is doing so people know whether to buy the shares. If you're a private company you don't have to tell anyone that. But if you decide to take your private company public, you do what's called an initial public offering or an IPO and you have to disclose all this information before you sell shares to the public."

"Right."

"So back in 2006, before the shit hits the fan with ABCP, Edenfree is making tons of money and so they decide, hey, let's take this company public. Let's do an IPO! And so they go out and hire a fancy law firm and start working on their prospectus, which is a big book that has all the information that someone thinking of buying shares in the company should know."

"Okay."

"Now listen carefully. In a prospectus, you have to make full and true disclosure of all material facts. A material fact is any fact that an investor might consider important when making an investment decision. If a fact is not material, you do not need to disclose it. There is a pant-load of law on this issue."

"Okay," I said.

Our wings arrived. I started to dig in. Dean just lit a cigarette.

"At the time of the IPO, in the summer of 2006, the ABCP market was rather hot and Edenfree's products were rated very highly by the ratings agencies for ABCP. The ratings agencies were all saying it was very low risk. But one of members of Edenfree's board, guy by the name of Wes Nolan, a very odd duck, was worried. Wes didn't trust the ratings agencies. He was reading a lot of things saying that the housing market in the United States was due for a correction and he was worried there could be a market disruption. That would mean that even a company like Edenfree that had little direct exposure to subprime might go down. Given these risks, Wes was worried that the price of the Edenfree's shares was too high, and so he hired Jay, one of the most prominent corporate and securities lawyers in Canada, to give him an opinion on whether he needed to make his opinion public."

"And Jay said he didn't have to do it?"

"Now listen carefully," Dean said. "At this point, Jay is not on for the shareholders of Edenfree. He's not on for the company, for the bank, or for the public. His client is this one director, okay?"

"Yes," I said.

"And the question is whether this one director has to disclose this opinion."

"Right."

"Well, Jay looked at the prospectus. And the prospectus talked about how there could be a housing bubble in the U.S. It talked about how much subprime Edenfree had. It talked about the risks of a general market disruption. It talked about the limited value of the ratings from the ratings agencies. In other words, the prospectus contained all the information upon which Wes had based his own opinion that Edenfree was being overvalued."

"Right," I said. "I think I see where you're going with this."

"So Jay said, as long as Wes wasn't forming his opinion of the price of Edenfree's shares based on information that was not publicly available, he didn't have to disclose it."

"I understand," I said.

"So this is a very hypothetical, weird thing to ask an opinion on. Like I said, Wes is a weird guy, he's paranoid about getting sued, he's a numbers guy, and so on. But, wouldn't you know it, next year, boom, the ABCP market freezes, Edenfree goes bust, and the OSC crawls right up everyone's butts for a whole host of other issues. Those issues got resolved, a few people got reprimanded and fined, and that was it."

"Okay," I said.

"But then, just this summer, the hacker group lulzsec hacks the bank that underwrote the IPO and releases about six terabytes of e-mails on Wikileaks. And lo and behold, the e-mails show that while the bank was going around pumping up Edenfree for the IPO, its proprietary traders were shorting the stock. That means betting it would go down."

"I know that," I said.

"So the OSC hits the roof. The bank is fucked, clearly, but the OSC also goes after everyone affiliated with Edenfree again. And they bring all the Edenfree guys in one after another for interviews and ask them: did you think the share price was overvalued? And all of them say no, are you kidding? I had my life savings invested in our stock. They all say that except for one. Wes. Who says, oh yeah, sure, I thought it was very overvalued. And they asked Wes, well, why didn't you say anything? And what does he say?"

"Okay, but ..."

"And all of a sudden," Dean cried, "Jay's this bad guy who tells board members to lie to the shareholders. Which …"

"But I mean, Dean, you gotta admit, it looks fucked up."

"Yeah," Dean said, "if you're an idiot!"

"No way," I said. "It's fucked up to advise someone they don't have to say anything when they think something they're selling is overvalued. I mean, even if that's the law, that's fucked up."

I looked at him, holding a wing in my saucy hands. I didn't want to piss him off, but I wanted to have my say too. Dean just looked out the window, his cigarette burning down between his fingers. Finally he looked back at me, and I saw that, yes, indeed, he was pissed off.

"All of the information," Dean said, "that was out there that led to Wes to form his opinion was available to these people. Did they read it? No. Did they think about it? No. They all ran out and bought stocks when they didn't know jack fucking shit about what they were buying. They just saw it on BNN and they thought it was money for nothing. And now it's Jay's fault they lost money? What the fuck is wrong with people? Why don't they think for themselves? Why are they so content to go along with things they don't understand?"

He paused, but of course I had nothing to say about that.

"And now these same assholes are ruining Jay's life, a guy who was not retained to represent their interests, and for what? For giving a legal opinion that was completely accurate?"

"All right man," I said.

"Stocks can go down as well as up," Dean said. "That's the chance you take. All right? Especially when you don't know what the fuck you're doing."

"All right," I said. "What do I know? You're right."

Dean shook his head. When he spoke next his voice was very bitter.

"I don't get it," he said. "I just don't understand people."

He barely had any wings. I tried to turn the conversation to happier subjects, but what were those? His personal life? Mine? Work? There wasn't even any basketball season coming up. It was like everything was turning into a minefield.

28

On Monday, I told Alan things were slowing down on the Goldstein file, and asked for new work. He turned me down and told me to bill the shit out of the Burke file. And that depressed me. It felt pointless to keep following Anthony. How could I prove that he wasn't cheating on his wife? And if he was cheating (which I doubted) how could I catch him when three other guys had failed?

I spent the whole week shadowing him, feeling vaguely like it had become my job to take advantage of a crazy woman. Eventually the day of the art show rolled around, and I found myself sitting at the patio of the Flatiron and the Firkin, across the street from the art gallery, wondering what to do with myself.

I had decided it was best if I didn't go to the art show; I'd stick out like a sore thumb. But I was frustrated with the lack of progress, so I figured 'what the fuck' and made my way over.

A waiter with a black shirt and white tie gave me a glass of red wine when I walked through the door. The place was packed with people standing shoulder to shoulder. I made my way straight to the cheese tray, drew upon my high school football experience to clear a little space, and started shoveling crackers into my mouth. My primary focus was this one particularly bad-ass cheese, like a soft Brie with blue powder sprinkled on it. Once satisfied, I got another glass of wine and squeezed my way through the crowd, looking at the paintings.

They were all, I shit you not, of dicks. Literal dicks. Like, penises. Each one was a close up of a dude's crotch, with the dick hauled out over the waistband and hanging down. Instead of being realistic, they were brightly coloured, blues and greens and pinks.

No price tags. I was looking around for someone to ask how much they cost, when I noticed the man himself coasting confidently towards me.

"Hi," he said. "My name is Anthony Burke. I'm the owner of this gallery."

I said: "I'm wondering how much these paintings cost."

He smiled:. "Because you want to buy one, or because you want to roll your eyes at how ridiculous modern art is?"

"What?" I said, offended. "I hope you don't think that just because I'm black, I came in here to make fun of your paintings."

"No," he said, "I think you're a private detective hired by my wife, and you came in here for the free cheese. You seemed to particularly enjoy the Cendrillon. Next time I recommend you pair it with a white."

"I don't know what you're talking about," I said.

"About the cheese, or my wife?"

"No," I said. "I understood the cheese. It was bitching."

"So we have similar tastes in at least one thing."

"And you know what, you got me," I said. "I did ask how much they cost because I'm going to make fun of modern art. But come on man. Tell me."

"I honestly can't tell you," Burke said. "Between you and me, the price is a bit fluid. Some of my customers, I have particular arrangements with, because I placed a piece with them before or something like that. You understand."

"Right," I said. I understood all right. He charged whatever the fuck he thought he could get away with and didn't tell anyone what that was.

"But," Burke continued. "These paintings are by a young British woman named Anna Herowicz, a painting in this series was on display at the Tait Modern in London, England, and these pieces sell in the, please don't sip your wine as I tell you this, the mid six figures."

It was good that he warned me. I would have spat out the wine for sure.

"Like," I said, "the multiple hundreds of dollars?"

"Yes," he said. "American dollars."

"Jesus fucking Christ man," I said.

He smiled a little, looking very relaxed.

"I'm sorry," I said. "I don't mean to piss off your customers."

"Oh, no one can hear you," he said, which was probably true, it was very loud in the small space. "And anyway they wouldn't care what you think. Just marks you as a no-nothing rube, that's all. Doesn't detract from the value of the art in the slightest. It might even increase it."

"How could it increase it" I asked, fascinated.

"Well," he said, "let's say you're very rich. At a certain point, it becomes difficult to impress your friends. Cars, houses, whatever. All that stuff is boring. Everyone has them. But art is different. If you buy a Herowicz, or let's say, a Hirst, or a Warhol, and you put that on your wall, all your friends are like 'oooh!' They know that you spent a ton of money for a picture of a dude's dick, or a bunch of random dots. So that means that, one, you're rich, and two, you're cultured. You're not some cheese-loving private detective who doesn't 'get it' and makes snarky comments like 'my kid could paint that!' You aren't just some nouveau riche clod who lucked into a fortune by managing a hedge fund or by founding a software company. You're a renaissance man. Do you see?"

"But it's just a picture of dude's cock!" I said.

"What's your name?" he asked me.

"Danny," I said.

"The thing is Danny," he said, "it doesn't matter what the art is. I mean, there are a billion examples. I assume you haven't heard of Felix-Gonzales Torres."

"You assume correctly, good sir."

"He's a very important contemporary artist, one of the top ten of the past fifty years, say. He had a work that was untitled but referred to as Lover Boys. It was 355 pounds of candy intended to be piled in one corner of a room in a pyramid and eaten by guests. It represented his lover's body wasting away from AIDS."

"What kind of candy?"

"It doesn't matter. Regular candy from the Bulk Barn. They were individual wrapped. We're talking a thousand dollars worth of regular candy or something."

"And it comes in a bag, or something?"

"Yeah," he said. "And then you make it into a pyramid in your house. It came with a certificate of authenticity. It was listed as a sculpture, described in a catalogue entry as 'dimensions variable'. Sold for $456,000."

"Jesus," I said.

"Another example. An art journalist owned a painting of Stalin by unknown artist. He bought for 200 British pounds. He says he puts it over his desk to inspire him in his work. Later he tries to sell it but no one wants to buy it. Maybe because, I don't know, it's a fucking portrait of the greatest mass murderer in history. So he gets his buddy, the well-known artist Damien Hirst, to paint a red nose on Stalin and sign it. They put it up for auction and estimated it would bring in 8,000 to 12,000 pounds. It sold for 140,000."

"Mondern art is fucked!" I exclaimed. "No offence, but my kid could paint this stuff! And I bet you that these people couldn't tell the difference."

"Well, sure," Burke said comfortably. "But art has always been about the brand of the artists, and not about the art itself. Now Van Gogh is a great artist. Your kid couldn't paint that. But can you really tell the difference between a lesser-known Van Gogh painting and a painting from one of his contemporaries? Let alone a skilled forgery. Can the people who pay big money for those paintings tell the difference? Hell, if someone didn't tell you the Mona Lisa was the best painting in the world, would it really grab your attention if you walked past it in the Louvre?"

Burke shrugged, then continued: "I like to think that some art is great and important and it will echo down through the generations, that it will speak to people outside of this place and time, that it really changes the people who experience it. But the business of art? The business? That's just branding."

"My buddy wouldn't like that," I said. "I have a friend that will only buy expensive things if he can tell the difference in a blind test."

It was the first thing I'd said that got a reaction from Burke. "Hmm?" he said, raising his eyebrows and looking a bit concerned.

"Yeah. So for example, he won't pay extra for a bottle of wine unless he can taste the difference himself from a cheaper bottle in a blind taste test. So I don't think he'd be into art. He'd probably want to look at the actual pictures without knowing who painted them. And I don't see how he could want to buy the bag of candy. He wouldn't even know that it was art, unless he saw the certificate of authenticity."

"He doesn't do that for everything though," Burke said.

"Really?"

"I think so," I said.

"Can I ask you something?"

"Sure."

"Is your friend lonely?"

The question surprised me so much I didn't know what to say. At first I opened my mouth to say, no, he's all right, but then I realized that Dean maybe was lonely.

Burke touched my shoulder.

"Do you smoke?" he said.

"No," I replied.

"Never mind. Come out with me."

We threaded our way through the crowded room, with Burke smiling and nodding at people and occasionally saying a word or two but pressing resolutely forward, and then we went through the back room (that was full of paintings covered in cloth and stacked on the floor) and headed outside into a little laneway, not wide enough for two cars to pass each other.

The building that housed the gallery was a 150-year-old brick warehouse on Front Street, now restored and occupied with cutesy restaurants and bars and luxury condos. A little to one side some guys were loading boxes of booze into a restaurant, while a waiter stood supervising and smoking.

Burke leaned up against the bricks and lit a cigarette. It was nice to be out in the quiet and the cool of the street.

"Why do you say he's lonely?" I asked.

"Well, a couple of things," Burke said. "First of all, brands are important to people. Maybe they shouldn't be, but they are. So if you ignore brands, out of principle or something, it seems like you're putting that principle above getting along with people. Do you know what I mean?"

I did. I just nodded.

"People care about brands. And so, to a certain extent, if you don't care about brands, you don't care about people."

I nodded again, and Burke took a drag on his cigarette.

"Second, and I guess more fundamentally, brands are important. You pointed out that you wouldn't even know that Lover

Boys was art unless it had a certificate of authenticity. That's true. But it's still art. It was the artist trying to send a message. And so if you lose the brand, if you only look at the thing itself, with no understanding of how that thing is viewed by other people, you lose something. You don't just lose all the stupid stuff, like a painting being worth more because Damien Hirst signed it. You also lose the message that can be there, that can really be there, in a bag of candy."

Burke looked off to the street and thought for a moment before he continued.

"A lot of people die of AIDS," Burke said. "Wasting away in the prime of their life. For what? For having sex? It reminds me of that quote by Phillip K. Dick, about people being punished entirely too much for what they did, for wanting to play. And that gradually disappearing pile of candy, if you think of it as a tribute to a dying man, so sweet and sad, it is a bit emotional. And you lose that in a blind test. $456,000? Well, all right, I guess I don't know. But you can't throw the baby out with the bathwater."

"He doesn't want to get caught up in all the bullshit," I said.

"Sure," Burke said. "And I understand that. It's a crazy world when you think that money could have bought AIDS medicine for 500 orphans in Africa and instead it got spent on candy. But life is bullshit, Danny. For all your guff about art, you strike me as a man that understands that. If you cut all the bullshit out of life, what are you left with?"

Burke waited for an answer. To give him credit, I think he was honestly giving me a chance to respond. Charming guy. Came across as genuine, like he actually cared about my friend who he'd never met. Smart and perceptive. Spoke slowly, with confidence. Warm. Right at that moment I realized he was cheating on his wife. And once I knew he had to be doing it, it was suddenly very easy to realize how. It had been in front of my face the whole time.

"Anyway," he said, "I better get back. Take care buddy."

"Okay," I said.

He went back inside and the door closed behind him. When I reached for the knob I realized there wasn't one. He'd locked me out. I laughed once, and it felt like a good release. I put my hand in my pocket and walked whistling up to Front Street.

29

When I got back to my office the phone rang. It was Tina. And she was crying.

"Was Dean with you last night?" she asked.

This inquiry really showed how nice and open Tina is. The typical wife who was worried her husband was cheating on her would not have asked the question in this fashion. She'd have said, "What were you up to last night?" in a fake cheery voice. Or she'd say: "Did you and Dean find any leads last night?" She wouldn't ask it in such a way that would immediately let me know that I should lie to cover for Dean.

So I didn't answer. Instead I just asked: "Tina, what's the matter?"

Another thing that showed what a nice person Tina was: she let it pass when I didn't answer the question. Most women who think they've been cheated on are like one of those little annoying dogs that won't give you the Frisbee back after you throw it to them.

"He's just so distant from me," she said. "It was supposed to be better when we came from California. But now it's just way worse with this stupid investigation. He's just so obsessed with it. And he barely touches me anymore. He doesn't look at me in the same way. I feel so fat and ugly."

"Tina, you're a total babe," I said. "Take my word for it. Look, I'll talk to Dean about it."

"No!" she said. "You can't tell him I called."

"Why not?" I said. "He won't be mad. I guarantee he doesn't even know how upset you are."

"Of course he knows," she said. "He just doesn't care."

"I'm sure he doesn't know, Tina."

"Well then don't tell him," Tina said. "I just thought he was so nice. He wasn't a dog like other men, always treating me like a piece of meat, always chasing around after other women. He was so polite and reserved. But now he's gone so cold. It's like he's not really here, he's always somewhere else. Tell me the truth Terrell: is there another woman?"

"No," I said. "There's no other woman."

"Are you sure?"

"How could I be sure? Maybe he's banging his secretary. If you want I can refer you to a private eye and they can follow him around. But I think that would be a waste of money. You said it yourself. He's not like other guys. He's having a tough year at work. That's all it is. Okay?"

After a pause, she said in a very small voice: "Okay."

"Are you sure you don't want me to call him?"

"No! I mean, yes, I'm sure, no I don't want you to call him."

"Well, all right. But keep your chin up Tina. It will be all right, I promise."

"Okay," she said. "Thanks Terrell. Come over and visit sometime."

"I will."

"I don't have any friends in Toronto; it would be good to see you."

"I'll be there sometime soon, for sure," I said. "Take care."

I hung up and called Dean.

"Hey bud," he said. "What's up?"

"I'm not supposed to be calling you," I said. "Tina just called me. She asked me if we were working together last night."

"Why'd she call you?" Dean asked.

"Well, I think she's worried you're cheating on her."

"Why's she worried about that?" Dean asked.

"I don't know," I said. "Have you been going out nights?"

"I've just been working late on some things."

"What are you working on?"

"Lawyer stuff," he said. "I've still got to work my regular job here."

And I wondered: did Dean just blow me off?
"Okay," I said, a bit hesitantly.

"Anyway," Dean said, "maybe she's right. I should spend more time at home."
"Are you feeling okay?" I asked.

"Well, I've felt better if that's what you mean," he said. "I'll be okay. I can do this. I should just get my head straight. Maybe you should come over for dinner."

"Sure, I'd like that. Are you free tonight?"
"Well, I've got a work thing," Dean said.
"Some other time I guess," I said.

"You know, you could just go visit Tina too. She doesn't have many friends in Toronto yet."
I grimaced, but I said: "Well, we'll see."
"Okay, I'll leave it to you. Let's talk soon buddy. Take care."

"Yeah, you too," I said, and hung up.

30

On the way home from work the next Monday I noticed I was being followed by a large black SUV, a Suburban. It wasn't exactly being subtle about it. By the time I got back to my apartment building it was so close if I'd stepped on my brakes abruptly it would have hit me. I parked and got out of my car and the Suburban parked two spots over.

I walked right up to it. The man that hopped out was a little taller than average, although not by much. He was not so much muscular as defined, cut like a diamond. Tendons formed hard lines under his skin. He was wearing a pair of very dark sunglasses and non-descript clothes that looked like they came from The Gap.

"Can I help you dude?" I said.

I meant to throw him off a bit, but he didn't say anything at all for a minute. His posture was very relaxed.

"Because, you know, you were following pretty …."

"I'm here to ask about a doctored comic book you tried to pass off as genuine," he said.

"I don't know what you're talking about," I said.

He smiled an empty, knowing smile.

"Don't you know lying just makes it worse?" he said. "The alterations to that comic book were designed to increase its value by tens of thousands of dollars. That makes you guilty of fraud over $5,000, which carries a maximum penalty of 10 years. Now, you won't get that much up here, of course, but you also attempted that crime in the state of Florida. They're a little sterner on the sentences down there. And you're an American citizen."

"Are you talking about the comic we sent to CQC?" I said. "Fucking get real. The whole point of CQC is to grade comics."

"You made a deliberate attempt to fool CQC."

"No I didn't," I said.

"Well, someone did. Where did you get the comic from?"

"I'm not telling you," I said. As I turned to go he darted forward and shoved my shoulder. It didn't look like much but there was a lot of force behind the short little blow and I lost my footing and stumbled down to the ground. "Hey," I said.

The guy took off his glasses and that's when I got scared. His eyes were very clear, almost colorless, and they were weak. He was blinking even in the dim light of the afternoon. But he was still very calm and quiet. There was absolutely no 'fight or flight' in his eyes, no adrenaline, no excitement. Pure business.

"I don't think you understand," he said.

"Smile!" someone called. It was Dean. He was walking towards us across the parking lot, holding up his phone. Then he stopped and started fiddling with it.

The guy crossed the distance to Dean in a few big strides, ripped the phone out of Dean's hands and threw it on the ground.

"Hey," Dean said. "My fucking phone."

"No pictures," the guy said.

"Well," Dean said. "I already e-mailed it to myself. So I'm not sure why you had to smash my phone."

I staggered up to my feet and hurried over.

"I know who you are," the guy said. "Mr. Mann."

"Well," Dean said. "You've got me at a disadvantage. Who are you?"

"That's not important," the guy said.

"You sure as shit aren't a private detective," Dean said. "You remind me of the guys we had guarding us when we were visiting gold mines in Tanzania. Are you ex-military? Blackwater?"

"I think you need to stop asking questions and start think about the kind of trouble you could get yourself in."

"Are you threatening me?" Dean said. "If so, cool. You can have my wallet."

"I don't want your wallet."

"Do you want information? Because if you're threatening me, I'll tell you whatever you want. I'll tell you I wear women's underwear if it makes you happy. Then I'll call the cops. As soon as I can find a payphone."

The guy still looked calm, but disgusted.

"Don't like lawyers, do you?" Dean said.

"No," he said. "I don't."

"Well, I guess that's why you came here first," Dean said.

"You know, you could get in a lot of trouble with the law society for submitting comics that you suspected ..."

"Oh, that he *suspected* now," I said.

The guy looked at me and I fell silent.

"Then call them," Dean said. "Go ahead and call them. I got your license plate in that picture, by the way. I take it the comic was significantly restored?"

The guy didn't say anything.

"Would you believe that's what we wanted to know?" Dean asked.

"So tell me where you got it," the man said. "This isn't a joke."

"No, it sure isn't," Dean said. "You're up here assaulting people? In daylight? They're freaking out down there, aren't they? Maybe we could help each other out?"

The guy smiled again. "You guys have a nice day," he said, and went back to his car. Dean and I were careful to get out of the way when he drove out.

"Jesus," I said. "That guy was intense."

"I agree."

"10,000 mile stare."

"Affirmative," Dean said, smiling a little.

"Do they do that every time they get a restored comic?"

"Nope," Dean said. "I'll bet you they don't. They pulled out the big guns for this one."

"Do you think the same thing happened to Brucie?" I said. Thinking: Maybe that guy is the murderer!

"Jesus, Terrell," Dean said. "We know for a fact it didn't happen because the clerk at the store told you he didn't know Brucie's real name."

"Oh yeah," I said.

"Anyway, I'm sure you're wondering how I knew to come here."

"Yeah."

"Well, Peter called me. Apparently that dude scared our names out of him. So I thought I'd stop by to warn you in person. Guess I showed up at the right time."

"Yeah," I said. "And it looks like we're back on the case."

"No kidding," he said, and looked at the wreckage of his phone. "The disbursements on this file are nothing to sneeze at."

31

The next morning Dean called and asked me whether I'd drive out to Over The Boards and have a chat with Mr. Ha.

"I was thinking about going with you," Dean said. "But here's the thing. I'm sort of working my way in with Vasily now."

"Like how?" I asked.

"Well, scalping tickets for one thing."

"Really?"

"Oh yeah," Dean said. "Right on Monday he e-mailed me to say he had some tickets for sale. I sent an e-mail around to everyone at the firm. No takers, so I knocked the price down and blew them out, then I made up the difference with Jay's money."

"Seriously?"

"Yeah," Dean said. "Now Vasily loves me. He's started e-mailing me about selling 'used' iPods, or trying to get people to invest in his schemes. The guy is a complete hustler. So, anyway, I've been thinking, Vasily doesn't know that I know you, right?"

"We showed up at poker together."

"But we didn't sit together. And we left at different times."

"Okay," I said.

"And when you went to visit Ha the first time, I wasn't there either."

"So?"

"So, maybe you should go see Mr. Ha on your own. Look, we know that Vasily and Ha know each other. I just think it's best for Ha to not know that I'm part of this investigation. That way he can't tell Vasily about me."

"Okay," I said. "What do you want me to say?"

"Just tell him the truth. That we bought a comic that was submitted through his store and that he sold online and it came back restored. He needs to tell us who submitted it."

"Okay," I said.

"Great. And call me right after, I'm really curious about this one."

I was at Over The Boards before lunch. As soon as Derek Ha laid eyes on me, I think he knew. He stiffened, his smile dropping away, and he looked back quickly to the family he was talking with. I wandered around the store, browsing through jerseys and studying signed photographs. For the first little while, Derek ignored me, but after about ten minutes I think it got unbearable for him, so he came over and said: "Can I help you?"

"Yeah," I said. "It's about the comic stuff again. Are you okay to talk here or do you want to go somewhere more private?"

He opened his mouth to say something, maybe that he had nothing to hide, or he resented the accusation or something like that, but then he closed it and turned around and walked away. I followed him through a door at the back into a little storeroom office, with big shelves crammed with boxes and a little desk with an old beige desktop computer.

Ha closed the door and looked at me.

"I bought an issue of Incredible Hulk #181 at Paradise Comics for $6,000." I said. "Previously, it had been sold on Heritage by this store, and it was submitted to CQC through this store's account."

"How could you possibly know that?" Ha interjected. He was speaking quickly and his whole bearing was stiff, like a little yappy dog. "That comic was probably submitted in hundreds of places over the world that year."

"We popped it out of the box and sent it down to CQC ..."

"Why would you do that?" Derek said.

"Never mind why," I said. "It came back restored."

"How do I know you didn't restore it yourself after you took it out of the box?" Derek cried. "You can't prove anything. I didn't do anything wrong. Anyway, I'm not responsible for CQC's rankings, or for my customers."

"Jesus," I said.

"Don't take the Lord's name in vain," Derek said. "Not in my store."

"Keep your voice down," I said. "Your customers can probably hear you."

Derek fell silent. He was literally quivering with emotion.

"Not only did it come back restored," I continued, "but CQC actually sent someone up to talk to me. Asking where the comic came from. For whatever reason, they were very, very concerned. Now, I didn't tell them anything. I thought I could come here and we could sort this out."

"So you're blackmailing me?" he said.

"I want information," I said. "Are you going to help me out here or not?"

He stared at me, still shaking with an emotion I thought was anger, and then his face crumpled like a baby's and he started to cry.

"I can't do this," Derek sobbed. "I can't go through this all again."

"Go through what all again?"

"What do you want from me?" he asked. "What do you really want? I don't have money, okay? I had to mortgage my home last time. Do you have any idea the kind of people you're messing with? Do you know what they'll do to me?"

His voice rose to a shriek during the last sentence.

I was so surprised I didn't say anything. Which was too bad, because maybe that was the moment. Maybe if I'd pushed him then, I could have gotten the information out of him, and things would have been different for everybody. But we don't always recognize those moments when they show up. Instead, I reached out to comfort him, to say, hey man, it's all right. But he jerked away from my hand.

"Get out of here!" he said. "Get out of my store, before I call the cops!"

"Mr. Ha," I started.

"I said get out!"

So I did. Everyone in the store (it was pretty busy) was perfectly motionless, staring at me like I'd just molested a cat. I hurried out, and in the parking lot I called Dean and told him what happened.

"I can't go through this again?" Dean asked.

"Yeah."

"That's what he said?"

"Yeah," I said. "Nuts, isn't it?"

There was a brief pause.

"Yeah," Dean said. "It sure is."

"What do you think it means?"

"I'm not sure."

"Well, what should we do now? I'm not really sure what our next move is. Do you think we should call the cops?"

"No!" Dean said. I was startled by the tone of his voice. "No, we don't want to do that."

"Why not?"

"We don't really have enough to prove anything yet."

"Yeah," I said, "but it's not necessarily our job to prove anything, right? We know a lot more than when we started. Detective Aston said that the case is still open. If we bring him all this stuff he might start working on it again."

"Look," Dean said. "It sounds like Ha is cracking. Give him a day to cool down. We'll drop by tomorrow and get the whole story. Once we know a little more, we can talk about whether we get the police involved. They're not going to do anything about it tonight anyway."

"Okay," I said. "If you say so."

And God help us, that's what we did.

32

I spent the next morning tailing Burke. Alan called me a little before lunch.

"Did you piss off the cops?" Alan asked. "Downloading kiddy porn? Something like that?"

"What?"

"A Detective Aston from homicide stopped by."

"Oh yeah," I said. "That's the guy who was on the Goldstein case. What did he want?"

"He's still here," Alan said. "He's asking all sorts of questions about what you were doing yesterday and last night. Won't say what it's about. I'm calling you from the bathroom. I told them I had to take a piss. What did you do yesterday?"

"Nothing," I said. "I interviewed a guy about the Goldstein case. Should I come in?"

"That's up to you," Alan said. "I told them you were unreachable."

"Thanks," I said, and hung up and went back to work.

A couple of hours later, after I'd mostly wrapped things up and was having a snack, I got a call from Dean.

"Detective Aston just left my office," he said.

"Alan told me he came looking for me," I said. "What's going on?"

"Are you sitting down?"

"What?"

"Are you?"

"Yes."

"Derek Ha is dead."

"What?"

"He jumped, or was thrown, off a bridge into traffic in Mississauga at 2 am."

"Oh, shit shit shit," I said. "Shit!"

"I know," Dean said.

"What did you tell him?"

"Nothing," Dean said. "He asked me some questions and I asked why he wanted to know. He said he wouldn't tell me, and so I said I wouldn't answer his questions. He got mad and threatened me. Finally he told me. I said, that's interesting, but I have no comment."

"You just stonewalled him?"

"Yeah, for now."

"But why?" I said.

"We have to keep this close, for just a little while," Dean said. "I think we're on the right path. If the cops start snooping around, anyone who might be involved with this will get spooked. They'll cover their tracks. I want them to think they're safe."

"But Dean, it's going to look as suspicious as hell if we don't talk to them."

"Of course it will," Dean said, "but so what? We didn't do anything. And even if we did, our decision to remain silent can't be mentioned if we're ever charged. They can be as suspicious as they like, but they can't do anything about it."

"Won't he charge you for obstructing justice or something?"

"What are you talking about? I have the right to remain silent."

"Dean, this is crazy," I said. "You're telling me a homicide detective walks into my office and you want me to exercise my right to remain silent?"

"That's exactly what I'm telling you," Dean said. "Terrell, trust me. You cannot hurt your position by just staying quiet. Okay? Just give me a bit more time to work on some leads. I don't want to risk what we've accomplished so far. I don't want this to end up like the thing from California. I just need a bit more time. All right?"

"Dean," I said, "I just don't see this. We should tell the cops everything."

"I need more time Terrell," he said. "I just need more time. Hang tight. I'm going to book an appointment with Oksana tonight. And I've got something planned about this CQC guy. I'm going to call you soon. Okay?"

I took my phone away from my ear and looked at it in disgust. Finally I put it back and said: "This is fucked up."

"Thanks," he said. "I appreciate it. It won't be long."

Try as I might, I just couldn't see things Dean's way. All I could think was that I really hoped this wasn't about the girl, and I really wished I wasn't so worried it was.

And now I didn't know where to go. I didn't feel like I could go home, or to work, because I was worried the cops would be waiting for me. So I decided to drive to Yonge and Lawrence and hang around in one of the parks up there. I took Avenue north, cranking Q107 and taking deep breaths, and that's when I noticed the black Suburban following me.

Mr. CQC mercenary, I thought. I felt a momentary chill. Could he have been the one to throw Ha to his death? But I knew Dean wanted to talk to him so I threw on my four-way flashers and pulled over to the side of the road, thinking he'd follow me and wouldn't have the balls to try anything right in the middle of a busy street.

But the black Suburban just rolled on by, and when I glanced at the driver through the window, I felt like I swallowed a cannonball. Because it wasn't the mercenary driving the car: it was Desean. And he never even glanced at me as he drove past.

My heart started beating so hard I was worried it might actually break or come loose or something. The taste in my mouth, bitter and metallic, was like I'd licked a battery. For a little while I was worried I was going to throw up. Eventually, I got myself together and drove up to Lawrence.

I parked my car at the public library and walked south to the park. I sat down on a bench and watched the people come and go. I couldn't live like this. People following me and threatening me and guys dying. You know how it felt? Lonely. That's how it feels when you do something you're guilty about. Like there's a barrier between you and everyone else. I felt envious of every single person walking past. Like they were all skipping along without a problem in the world.

And some of it must have shown on my face, because when the mercenary suddenly sat down next to me, he said: "Terrell, you look like a man with the weight of the world on your shoulders."

33

I picked up Dean at his house at eight pm that night.

"How did you set up this meeting?" I asked. "Did you do it through Milo?"

"No," Dean said. "We're going to her place."

"How did you get her address?" I asked.

"She e-mailed me about some legal stuff. Basically she wants immigration advice. I've been talking to her a bit. I told her I needed to talk to her in person so she invited us over."

"I didn't know that," I said.

Dean shrugged.

"Is that where you've been going at night?" I asked.

"You sound like my wife," he said. "What about this thing with the CQC guy?"

"He said his name was Tom," I said. "I arranged to meet him tomorrow at one pm at the Starbucks at King and Yonge."

"Great work," Dean said.

"Dude, I gotta tell you, I was a bit freaked out when I found out Desean was following me."

"No kidding," Dean said. "We'll take care of this soon, I promise. For now, keep it tight."

"Okay," I said.

Oksana lived in the northwest corner of the city, at Jane and Finch. It's one of the most notoriously violent neighborhoods in Toronto, which actually isn't saying too much, not compared to New Orleans anyway. Just a lot of old high rise apartment buildings and poor immigrants.

The lobby of Oksana's building smelled like stale food and the buzzer was broken. We rode the elevator up to the eleventh floor and then knocked at her door while people shouted at each other down the hall.

The door opened, revealing Oksana dressed in a bathrobe, done up loosely enough so that I could see the side of her breast. She didn't say anything, only motioned for us to come in.

Nicely decorated place. An Indian rug on the floor, potted plants, goldfish in a little glass bowl. Laminated posters of famous paintings on the walls, and a metal wine rack in the corner. Looked like the apartment of a classy young undergraduate.

Oksana glided over to the couch and sat down. Dean and I pulled up chairs from the dining table.

"So," Oksana said, "is it just more questions or do you want to do anything this time?"

"Can I smoke?" Dean asked, taking out his cigarettes.

"What do you want? You know it is not safe for me to talk of my work. Desean has informants in this building. Why are you doing this to me?"

Dean got his cigarette going. "When we got the bill for the last time we had one of these little chats it cost $1,000 and it was payable to some fishing store on Sheppard," Dean said. "So how come every time Brucie hired you it was $2,000, and it was payable to some random Moneris machine?"

Oksana lowered her big eyes.

"I don't know," she whispered. "Maybe Desean …"

"No way," Dean said. "You said that Brucie showed up outside the Rail and you gave him your contact info. He didn't make contact with you through the regular channels. You knew he was a dumb kid and he was infatuated with you, and so you ran a scam on him. Let me guess how it worked. You had a friend of yours hire you for the night by paying the regular rate to the fishing store. When Brucie showed up, you charged him $2,000 through your friend's Moneris machine, and then you and your friend split the difference. Is that about right?"

"When I saw you in the club," Oksana said, "and you said his name, you said Brucie, I was so afraid. I thought that Desean would hear. That he would find out what I had done."

"Who was your partner?"

"I cannot say," she said.

"Was it Vasily Bogdanov?" Dean asked.

That startled her. She nodded.

"How did you know?" she asked.

"Did Vasily ever meet Brucie?"

"Of course," Orkana said. "Every time. So he could run through the credit card. Vasily loved Brucie. He used to joke with him, to tell him stories. He called him Young Master Goldstein. He told him jokes about Jews and lawyers. He said I was teaching him to be a man. Afterwards Vasily would pay me in cash."

"Did they ever talk about comics?"

"No," Oksana said. "Vasily does not care about comics. He is a man. Brucie is a boy. I don't understand why you ask about comics. Brucie was just a boy. When his money ran out, I thought he would learn his lesson. I thought he would be sad and then find a nice girl. I did not know he would kill himself."

"Now this is important," Dean said. "Did Vasily ever say anything about Brucie after the last time you saw him? He didn't mention anything about comics or money or Brucie or anything?"

"No, no," Oksana said. "I told you. Brucie said he would get more money. But then he did not come around anymore. I thought he went to school."

Dean kept looking at her. He did not say anything.

"You can't tell anyone about this," Oksana said. "If you tell Desean, things will be worse for me."

"We won't tell him," Dean said.

"Please," Oksana said. "I should not have done it. If you keep asking questions, anything might happen."

"You'll be safe," Dean said. "I promise."

He paused for a moment, and then he leaned forward and took her hands. When he resumed speaking he looked straight into her eyes. "You know, Terrell and I did something like this once before. In California. It was about a girl kind of like you. We were … we were too late. I was too late. I didn't take care. I won't let that happen with you. Do you understand? I have fucked up a lot of things over the years, but the thing in California is the biggest regret of my whole life. I won't let it happen again with you. No matter what. You'll be safe. I promise."

Oksana and Dean had what you might call a moment. And then we left. Dean said to me:

"We should be careful when and where we meet from now on. If Desean's following you, and he sees us together, it could blow our chance to get to the bottom of this."

Careful about her? What about me? I barely said two words to Dean all the way home, but he didn't even seem to notice I was pissed.

34

While I was walking to the front door of my apartment building, a voice spoke to me from the bushes.

"Mr. Delacroix?"

I jumped and turned. A man was walking towards me. Little guy, unibrow, muscular.

"Who are you?" I asked.

"Detective Aston," he said, and held up his badge for me to inspect. "You need to come down to the station with me right now. I'm parked around back."

When I got to the station, they took my Blackberry and put me in one of those grim windowless rooms with a mirror along the wall like you see in the movies. I sat there for about half an hour, getting more and more nervous, and more and more angry at Dean. This was such bullshit. Here I was, a private detective, somebody who had to stay on good terms with the police, and now I was a goddamn murder suspect. Why? Because I couldn't tell the truth about our investigation. Why? Because Dean was into some girl or thought he could do this by himself? It was a load of crap.

The door opened and Aston came in.

"Do you know why you're here, Delacroix?" he said.

"No," I replied.

"I don't believe you," he said. "I've got a roomful of witnesses that put you in Ha's store the day before he fell to his death. Now I've got you avoiding me. How do you think that looks to me?"

"I didn't do anything," I said.

"Witnesses say that Ha was screaming at you to get out, that he'd call the police. What were you talking about?"

"Nothing," I said.

"Nothing?" he said.

"It was part of an investigation."

"So what?" he said. "You think that makes it confidential? You think you don't have to answer my questions because it was part of your investigation? Think again, bud. You're going to have to explain what you were doing in there."

I shook my head.

"Where were you at two am this morning?

"At home."

"Oh, were you?"

"Yes."

"Home alone, huh?"

"Yes."

"So when Mr. Ha told his wife he's gotta go out and meet someone, and that's why he's leaving at such a late hour, guess he wasn't talking about you, was he?"

"No," I said.

"Even though she specifically mentioned your name?"

"What?" I said. "I never went to go meet him. I was at home in bed."

"Well, that's what she said. You calling her a liar?"

"I was home in bed at two this morning," I said. Sweat was pricking through the back of my shirt. I could barely breathe.

"And what about this?" Aston said, and slapped down a piece of paper on the table.

It was a photocopy of a note that read:

I KNOW WHAT YOU DID TO PAY THE RENT DURING THE LOCKOUT.

"Is that what you wanted to talk to Ha about?" Aston said. "How he paid the rent during the lockout?"

"I've never seen this before," I said.

"Do you know how fucked you are right now?" Aston said. "We've got you swearing and yelling at Ha the day before he dies. We've got his wife saying you're going out to meet him the night he dies. We've got you investigating some other mysterious death by falling from a few weeks back. How do you think ..."

And then my iPhone rang. It was tucked in my front shirt pocket and I'd forgotten about it.

"Don't answer that," he said.

I took it out to turn it off and I saw it was Dean. Inspiration hit me.

"It's my lawyer," I said. "I'm allowed to talk to my lawyer."

"You watch too much TV!" he said. "You're talking to me right now."

He tried to snatch the phone away but I leaned back and put it to my ear.

"Dean, I'm in the police station," I said. "I'm under arrest."

"What are you under arrest for?" Dean said.

I noticed that Aston had put his hands down on the table and was just glaring at me.

"I don't know."

"How could you not know? What did the cop tell you?"

"He didn't tell me anything."

Dean paused. When he spoke again, his voice was tightly controlled.

"Are you sure you're under arrest?"

"What? Yeah. He said I had to come down with him."

There was another moment of silence.

"Is he there?"

"Yes?"

"Ask him if you're under arrest."

I looked at Aston.

"Am I under arrest?"

"That's the least of your worries," he said.

"Jesus wept," Dean said bitterly in my ear.

"You're looking at some serious trouble right now, Terrell," Aston said.

"Get the fuck out of there," Dean told me.

"I can't just leave."

"Really?" Dean shouted at me. "Did you try asking that?"

I looked at Aston.

"Can I go now?"

"I don't think you understand the gravity of your situation, Terrell," Aston said. "Let me spell it out for you and your lawyer again."

"Can you go, yes or no?" Dean said. "Ask him, for God's sake."

"Yes or no?" I said.

"You can go when we say you can go," Aston said.

"Okay," Dean said. "Terrell, from now on, the only sentence that leaves your mouth, the only sentence, is 'can I go now.' Understood? Not one other word. Not if he says, just tell me this one thing, not if he says, you need to just fill out this one form, not ever. Okay? Keep your teeth pressed together unless you are asking him if you can go. Understand?"

"Yes," I said.

"Now give him the phone. If he hangs up, remember what I told you."

I passed the phone to Aston, who was now smiling like the cat that got the canary. "Dean-o," he said. Then he waited for a while. "Well, can't blame me for trying, can you?" Another pause. "Well, I guess that will be for a court to decide. Usually, they don't blame me for trying either." Now just a brief hesitation. "You have a nice day." He hung up.

For a while we looked at each other, and I could tell he was gauging how much more he could get away with.

"Let me just ask you one more thing," he said. "And then I'll let you go. What's the deal with this lockout talk?"

I said nothing.

"Come on now. How do you think this is going to end? You think with all the evidence we've got on you, you're just going to walk away? Terrell, I think you're just a pawn in all of this. I really do. I think you're taking orders from your lawyer buddy. I think he treats you like you're stupid. Well, you know what? Maybe he's right. Because you're the one holding the bag here, Terrell. Not him. You're the one we've got the dirt on. And is Dean really looking out for you? Or is he looking out for himself, or for some other people that I don't know about? Does keeping quiet protect you, or them? Hmm? You start talking now, and we can go easy on you. You clam up, well, the hammer will fall on whoever the hammer can reach. And from where I'm sitting, the closest one is you."

He might have had me if he'd started with that tack. But I was pissed at him for tricking me. I was as embarrassed as fuck, to tell you the truth. So I heeded Dean's commandment and said: "Can I go now?"

"Sure you can," Aston said. "You always could. Have a nice night."

35

I stood at the corner outside, wondering how I was going to get home, listening to the sounds of people laughing and drinking on the patio across the street. A queasy feeling, like a snake coated in oil turning itself into a knot, was moving through my stomach. Part of me just wanted to take the subway home, but that would only be delaying the inevitable.

I called Dean.

"Are you out?" he said.

"Yes," I replied.

"Okay," Dean said. "If you see him again, ask if you are under arrest. If so, ask what for. Then call me. All right?"

"I didn't tell him anything,"

"I bet you told him more than you thought," Dean said.

"No," I said. "He asked me what I said to Ha and I wouldn't tell him."

"Oh really?" Dean said. "So I guess that means you told him you did visit Ha. That you did talk to him. Maybe even that Ha was yelling at you. Maybe even that it was for an investigation. Right?"

"He knew that already."

"No," Dean said. "He pretended like he knew, so you would confirm it."

"Whatever," I said. "That doesn't matter. What does matter is that Ha's wife said Ha told her he was going out to meet me late at night. Why would he say that?"

Dean was losing his patience.

"Why would he say that? Gee, I don't know. Maybe Aston lied to you. Did that ever occur to you?"

"Cops can't lie to you."

"For sure they can," Dean said. "They do it all the time. The Supreme Court of Canada has ruled that they can keep pressuring you after you've expressed your desire to exercise your right to remain silent. They've ruled that confessions prompted by police lies are admissible. But they've also consistently ruled that an accused person's decision to exercise their right to remain silent can't be held against them in court. It can't even be mentioned. Terrell, I told you that. Remember? Why didn't you ask to call me as soon as they picked you up?"

"What the fuck man?" I said. "This is bullshit. It's not my job to blow off the cops. All right? They're trying to find out what happened to Ha. They're the good guys! Why am I trying to hide shit from them, especially when I've got Desean following me around?"

"Because if we tell Aston what we know, he's going to go pick up Vasily and try the same thing with him as he did with you. That's his shtick and 90% of the time it works. It worked on you. But it won't work on Vasily. He'll clam up like nobody's business. He won't sit there sweating and making denials. And then he'll walk out and he'll be gone."

"Is this about the girl?" I said.
"What?"
"It is, isn't it? You want to keep Oksana out of it."
"Sure," Dean said. "That's another thing."
"Dean, why are you worrying about her more than me?"

There was a pause, and for a moment, I thought I'd gotten through to him. But when he spoke, his voice was strained, and I realized that he was just trying to gather himself:
"I'll talk to you tomorrow," he said. "Have a good night."

Then he hung up.

36

Tom the mercenary was late getting to the meeting, but I had the feeling he'd been watching us for some time. He ordered an herbal tea. I ordered a big fucking Latte, with caramel and chunks of salt. I had a vague sense that I'd earned it. Dean had a black coffee.

"So let me tell you how we can do this," Dean said. "We're more than happy to share what we know with you."

At this I had to bite my tongue. I couldn't believe we were working with this guy instead of the cops.

"But first you have to tell us what brings you here. Okay? Nothing about who employed you, or whatever, but we really need to know everything you know. Then we'll do the same. Then maybe we'll be able to help each other out a bit. I don't think our goals are mutually exclusive."

"You boys don't want to get the police involved?" Tom asked.

"No, not yet," Dean said. "I think this situation needs a bit of subtlety right now. I don't want to warn off the people who are responsible for what we're looking into."

Tom looked at us carefully, smiling his little Mona Lisa smile.

"And," Dean continued, "I don't think your employer wants this shit in the papers either. Am I right?"

Tom didn't answer that. Instead he said:

"Well, back in late July, I have reason to believe that CQC received a comic that had been very subtly and very thoroughly restored. We're not talking just a little microtrimming. Someone had taken the item from about a 4.0 to a 9.2. Colored pencils, Japan tape, the whole works. Real professional job. It was the trimming that got caught. CQC has been very sensitive about that kind of thing since 2005."

"Right," Dean said.

"Of course, it's not a crime to submit a restored book," Tom continued. "The person submitting it might not know it's restored, or might want it graded even if he does know, although the usual courtesy would be to let CQC know what you're giving them. But like I said, this was a real professional job and so CQC made some routine inquiries of the account holder. The store clerk said he had no idea who submitted it. Never seen the kid before. Paid in cash. No driver's licence. Phony name on the form."

"So CQC took note," Dean said.

"A couple of weeks ago, another restored book comes in," Tom said. "Same thing. Microtrimming sets off the alarm. The rest of the book is completely redone, but so cleverly that it fooled one of the three graders, even though he was on the lookout for it. Consensus is: this comic was restored by the same individual as the first one. This eventually led to my visit to Peter at Paradise Comics. Peter said you were investigating the death of one of his customers. Boy by the name of Brucie Goldstein, who fit the description of the kid who submitted the first comic. Pete also told us that you submitted that comic immediately after buying it already sealed inside a CQC box."

"Meaning that the comic had already fooled CQC once. So let me guess. The client hit the roof and you abandoned all subtlety."

Tom smiled his prissy smile.

"Now tell me your side of the story," he said, and took out a pad of paper upon which he was apparently going to take notes.

"Well, Brucie died on August 25 by falling off of a bridge," Dean said. "We searched his room and we find two items of interest: an old-fashioned electronic tracking device and an empty CQC box."

Dean set it down on the table. Tom checked it out, front and back.

"Detective Comics," he said.

"Right," Dean said. "And we ask ourselves: why would he take it out of the box? To resubmit it, we eventually decide. So we look around, we heard about how he submitted it, paid cash, gave a fake name. It came back restored. So we figured, he restored the comic, it didn't work, he killed himself. Because he needed money, you see. He'd been seeing this Russian escort and he was in love with her and he'd run up a big bill on his credit card."

Tom nodded.

"But something didn't jive about that," Dean said. "Because before he bought the comic, he'd provided Peter with a short list of comics, and we didn't know why he was interested in those particular comics. And we started to think that maybe all the comics on the list had been submitted to CQC through a store called Over the Boards, a hockey memorabilia store that only had a CQC account for one year. The store is owned by a guy named Derek Ha."

"Right," Tom said.

"So what if he had, for some reason, been looking for comics in that particular store? Based on that assumption, we spent the money to buy another comic off Brucie's list. We resubmitted it, it came back restored. And apparently, according to you, it came back restored the same way as Brucie's comic."

"So you think he bought the comic because he knew it was restored? And sent it back to CQC to prove it?" Tom said.

"It's possible, yes."

"Why do you think he did that?" Tom said.

"Blackmail," Dean said.

"You think he was blackmailing Derek Ha?" Tom asked.

"Yeah, I do," Dean said. "We know for a fact that one day in August Brucie borrowed a car from his acquaintance of his, and did a quick switch in a parking garage, like he was trying to shake someone who was following him. Also, when Terrell visited Derek Ha to talk about this, Ha started freaking out, saying he couldn't go through this again, and that we didn't know what 'these people' were capable of. Then he clammed up. The next morning, Derek Ha is found dead after falling off a bridge. The cops picked up Terrell last night and tried to shake some information out of him. The detective let it slip that they'd found a note threatening Derek Ha. They accused Terrell of sending it. But I think that note was left over from the summer. I think Brucie might have sent it. So I had my firm do some property searches, and guess what came up?

Derek Ha put a $250,000 mortgage on his house in mid-August. Right after Brucie found out the comic was restored."

Dean waited for a moment while Tom took all that down.

"Interesting theory," Tom said. "But how would Brucie have known the comic was restored?"

"Well," Dean said. "I don't know. But I spoke to Oksana last night."

"This is the hooker?"

"Yeah," Dean said. "And here's the scam she was running. This guy Vasily Bogdanov was one of her customers. On nights the kid wanted to see her, Vasily would hire her for her usual rate of $1,000. Then they would charge the kid $2,000 and split the difference between them. But the weird thing is, this Vasily guy is a Russian NHL agent, and he works with Over The Boards all the time. Getting them signed merchandise."

Tom was taking notes furiously.

"So this guy Vasily is connected both with Over The Boards and with Brucie," Dean said. "Our tentative theory is that Vasily was the one to submit the forged comics to CQC through Over The Boards. Then he let his little scam slip to Brucie, boasting about what a big deal he is. And Brucie saw an opportunity. He bought a comic that had been submitted to CQC through Over The Boards. He resubmitted it. This time CQC caught it because they were on the lookout for microtrimming. Then Brucie blackmailed Derek Ha, and he picked up the money. But there was a tracking device in it and they followed him back to his house. They called him up and threatened him. He came out with the money. And then they threw him off the bridge. And then, after we show up at Over The Boards, they did the same thing to Derek Ha."

"Nice theory," Tom said. "But you've got no proof."

And he smiled again, that thin, superior smile, like a librarian smiling at a student that had mispronounced a word.

"So that's where I come in, correct?" Tom said.

"See what you can dig up on this guy," Dean said. "That's the deal."

"I can make inquiries," Tom said. "The question is, what do you bring to the table? Maybe after this little tete-a-tete, we should just go our separate ways."

"Simple," Dean said. "I'm in with Vasily. He's got me working as his fence."

To prove this, Dean opened his briefcase and dumped a bunch of iPods onto the table. They were still boxed and shrink-wrapped, but the writing on the boxes was in Spanish.

"I paid $100 each, but no one wants them and I've got to blow them out."

Tom looked at them, his smile gone, and said: "I'll give you $100 for three."

"Done."

"Will you take American?"

"Does the Pope shit in the woods?"

A lot of people watched as this transaction was carried out.

"Anyone else?" Dean asked, and they looked away. He looked back at Tom. "You want to make a move on Vasily, you're going to need me."

"Okay," Tom said. "Well, I think we understand each other." He sipped his tea and looked at the iPods. "You know what you should do with those, is send them over to our troops in Afghanistan. They'd go wild to get something like that over there."

"I'll consider it."

"Those troops need your support," Tom said. "They're fighting for our freedom."

"Duly noted," Dean said, and stood up. "I'm guessing you know how to get in touch with us. Want to leave a number so we can get in touch with you?"

"Nope," Tom said.

"Didn't think so. Think about it bud. I've already half-hatched a scheme to bust this dude. But I need your help to make it work."

Dean motioned to me with his head.

"Come on, let's go."

Outside, I said:

"Why didn't you tell me all your fancy theories?"

"I just did," he said.

"You told me at the same time as that psycho? I didn't even say two words in there."

"Look," Dean said. "It's just my theory. Okay?"

"And the less I know, the less I can spill to the cops, is that right?"

"It's not like that."

"You don't trust me!" I said. "After all this, you don't trust me. You probably don't even need me any more now that you've got your black ops buddy in there."

"Fuck Terrell," Dean said. "Why are you acting like this? You sound like Tina. You've done lots for this case. You found the letter, you set up this meeting. God."

"I just can't believe how you hide things from me."

"I'm not hiding things from you," he said. "I'm just thinking about them."

"I don't think you trust me."

Finally Dean rounded on me.

"I told you not to talk to the cops," Dean said, "and you talked to the cops."

"It's not my ..."

"I don't want to hear your excuses," Dean said. "It's fine. Okay? It was a tough situation and I don't blame you. But this is not going to go down like the thing did in California."

"You're blaming that on me?"

"Of course not! Jesus! This isn't about you Terrell, it's about me! Okay? You're fine. You're doing great. But Tanya was on me, and so is this one, and that means I can't just hand things off to other people and hope they go okay. All right? And if you want to take that all personally, and say I don't trust you, well there's nothing I can do about that."

He looked anguished. Now I felt guilty, as well as pissed off.

"You're nuts," I said. I meant it to sound funny, like a peace offering, but it didn't.

"Whatever," he said. "I'll call you when Tom gets back to me. It won't be long."

He turned and walked away. I watched him go. Part of me wanted to run and catch up with him, but I didn't.

37

When I got back to the office, I got a call from Dean's home number. I almost didn't answer it, but it's not my nature to sulk. I picked it up and said:

"Yo," I said.

"I'm going to leave Dean," Tina said. She was sobbing. "I'm going to go back to California. I just wanted to say good bye."

"What?" I said. "No, Tina. Don't do this."

"He was out again last night, investigating, he says."

"I was with him," I said. "He was investigating."

"Where were you?"

"We were interviewing this girl," I said. "A Russian hooker who knew Brucie, the kid that killed himself."

After a moment of silence she said, flatly, not crying: "He told me you were visiting comic stores."

Well Dean, I thought, not even you could blame me for that one. You've got to give me a heads up on this stuff.

"Oh," I said, "well, we checked out some comic stores too."

"Don't you lie to me too," Tina said. "You're my only friend up here. I don't have anything to do all day. I just sit around alone. I miss all our old friends from California. I just feel so bad all the time. Dean doesn't even touch me."

"Tina," I said. "It's okay! Everything's okay."

"Not even my daughter loves me anymore," Tina sobbed. "She doesn't respect me because she's doing so well at school. I'm scared the neighbors know about me. The man across the street always stares at me."

"Well, of course he does," I said. "You're a beautiful woman."

She snuffled. "No, I'm not."

"What are you talking about?" I said. "You're totally hot. You're a MILF."

That made her laugh a little.

"Who is this Russian prostitute?"

"Just a hooker that Brucie was seeing before he killed himself."

"Why didn't Dean tell me about her?"

"I don't know," I said. "You'll have to ask him."

"Can I be honest?" she said. "I wish that he was infatuated with some Russian hooker. So that I had a rival for his affections. Because, that way, he would at least have affections. That I could get."

At the end of the sentence she was tearing up a bit.

"But I think he's damaged or something," she continued. "I think he's been faking it with me for a long time. Maybe since the beginning. Maybe he was only ever grateful for helping him get clean. Maybe he's only staying with me because he feels like he owes it to me."

"That's crazy," I said. It was, in fact, not crazy at all. Hearing her say it made me cold. I did not think it would go well for Dean if he came home to an empty house that night. "Look, I'm the last one to talk about working harder in your relationships. But I can tell you I have regrets about my ex-wife. I don't regret that it didn't work out, but I wish I'd worked harder at it. I wish I'd earned my way out, like Dr. Phil said."

"I've earned it," she said. "I've earned my right to leave. You don't have to tell me what Dr. Phil says. I still watch him, even if my husband and daughter are too good for him."

"Well," I said, and then I trailed off. What was there to say?

"Why didn't you ever come over and visit, Terrell?"

"Just busy."

"Busy with what?"

"My regular life."

"Well, goodbye," she said.

"What do you mean goodbye?"

"Well, I'm going."

"Tina, don't go. Try to talk it out with Dean."

"I'm done talking with him," she said. "I tried all I can."

"Why don't you call him?"

"No," Tina said. She'd calmed down. "I'm leaving. I'll call him from California. We can figure it out there."

"Okay," I said.

"Why don't you come over for a drink, Terrell?" she said. "It would be nice to see you one last time before I left."

"All right," I said. "I'll be there in twenty minutes."

Now it would be easy for me to say I went over there with the intention of talking her out of it. And I kind of did. But on some level, I knew. It was all happening by reflex, by automatic process, but that's not an excuse.

In her prime, Tina had been what you might call 'stacked.' Tall, almost six feet, with spectacular natural breasts, big hips, and big shoulders too.

Now, after the two kids, and a few years of retirement, she'd gained between ten and twenty pounds. She had space for it, but I could definitely notice it, as I bent her over the bathroom sink and jammed her from behind, a fistful of her fragrant blond hair in my hand.

She moaned and shrieked and we watched ourselves in the mirror. We looked just like what we were: a couple of porn stars who were getting a little long in the tooth. But it felt good, to just let go, to stop thinking, stop worrying, to let it all go.

38

When we were done she seemed to be in a good mood. I had to get out of there because I didn't want her to see the guilt in my eyes. We hugged and kissed and she whispered in my ear, and then I was out the door and back in my car.

Sex. There are a few precious moments when everything feels okay, when you're locked into the present. But then that passes, and everything comes rushing back in, everything you forgot about for a little while, along with one more thing to worry about. I felt like that was the story of my whole life, just adding the links to my chains, one after another, like Jacob Marley in A Christmas Carol.

The next morning I called Mrs. Burke and asked if she was available to come in for a chat.

"Has there been a development in the case?" she asked.

"I just want to talk to you about some things, in person, if possible."

She didn't like that but eventually she agreed to come in on Monday.

Later that afternoon Dean called me.

"Hey man," he said. "Tom wants us to meet him at his hotel by the airport."

"Okay," I said. Just the sound of his voice made me feel sick. "What time?"

"I said two pm so we could beat traffic. I've got the car so I'll pick you up at your work."

"Okay."

The first thing he said when I got in the car was:

"Look, I'm sorry about the other night. I really lost my temper. I thought about it and I was out of line."

"It's okay," I said. "But I'm still not sure I've forgiven you for letting Desean follow me around."

"Well," Dean said, "I'm not sure I've forgiven you for fucking my wife."

He glanced at me out of the corner of his eye, and he must have seen the anguish in my face, because the next thing he said was: "I'm sorry."

Then he laughed, and said: "Jesus, why am I sorry?"

And I started to cry. It was not a manly sight, or a pretty one. I am not a pretty crier. Snot was coming out of my nose even faster than the tears were coming out of my eyes. I started to quake like a jell-o statue. Big noisy sobs. You get the picture. I just felt like my whole shitty life had driven me to this point.

"Sure," Dean said. His voice wasn't hard or cruel, it was just extremely tired. "You get to cry. Of course. She cries, you cry. Why don't I get to cry?"

"I'm sorry," I said. "It just happened."

"People always say that. How do these things just happen for you? They are so difficult for me."

I was still crying, but more quietly now. I couldn't look at him, so I stared between my feet at the mat on the floor. If I could have been sent anywhere else in the world, I would have taken it. But there wasn't any escape.

After a moment, Dean spoke:

"Can I be blunt? It did not just happen. It was your fault. You shouldn't have done it. But you did not sneak in there and bust up this awesome relationship with your amazing seducing skills. It is my fault it came to this. I knew something was going to happen."

"Why?" I asked. My voice was still a little raw.

Dean shrugged, and smiled his smile that was like a little wince.

"Well. I met up with Tina when I'd been clean for eight weeks. I started looking after her kid, going to parent teacher meetings, she was supporting me through law school. And I really loved her, and I thought I could give her what she needed. But here is the thing. I can have sex with her, I can be kind to her; I can listen to her bitch about the neighbors, her family, and her coworkers for hours on end. I can be a father to her daughter and to our son. I can give her my money, I can cook us nice dinners at night. I can show up to her with social functions. But I can't feel passionate about her, Terrell. That's not just a switch I can throw. No matter how much I want to. And I can only fake it for so long, until it becomes clear to her that I'm just going through the motions. I wish I could do it Terrell. I really, really do. But I can't. I just can't."

I was wiping my face, trying to clean up.

"I'm sorry man," I said again.

"Yeah," he said. "I'm sorry too."

We drove without saying anything for about one song on the radio, and then I said, out of the blue:

"Do you ever think the blind taste testing is a bad idea?"

"What?" he said.

"Do you ever think that you should stop it?"

"What does that have to do with anything?"

"I was talking about it with some guy, and he didn't think it was a good idea."

"Well, I don't know what you mean. I like it to do it. I think it's important. But it's not for everyone. I had this buddy that wouldn't drink McDonald's coffee. He said he could taste the additives and chemicals. He swore by the stuff he got at this little independent café. I was like, bullshit. I took him to McDonalds and he spat it out, made this face. So one day I switched his coffee."

"Did he notice?'

"Yeah, he said, which one is this? I told him it was a new thing, shade-grown Ugandan. He told me it was great."

"What did he say when you told him the truth?"

"I didn't have the heart."

"What?"

"Partially I didn't want to make him feel stupid. Even though he was stupid. But it was more than that. His identity as a person who insisted on superior coffee was important to him. If I told him the truth he wouldn't just feel stupid. It would shake his whole world, in a little way. I guess I should have done it. The guy was living a lie. Right? He should know that. The same way I should tell him if I knew, say, his wife was cheating on him, even though it wouldn't make him happy. But I didn't. I let him go on believing what he wanted to."

We didn't say anything the rest of the way.

39

The hotel was massive, one of those new monstrosities that have sprouted up like Triffids in Toronto's suburbs. Vaguely modern aesthetic, with smart floors and neat paintings on the walls, but the overwhelming impression was of bland empty space. No one was even near us as we walked to the elevator.

Absolutely nothing I saw anywhere in Tom's hotel room betrayed the nature of its occupant. The two twin beds were both made and there were no clothes in sight, no novels, no leftover takeout food. A black rolling suitcase and a black carryon bag, both zipped closed. That was it.

I sat down at the little round table near the window, and Tom and Dean sat across from me.

"So what have you got for us?" Dean asked.
Tom motioned to three plain file folders sitting on his desk. "I have some friends who ran a few searches. Let's start with Vasily Bogdanov."

He opened the first folder. "Here in Canada he was charged with impaired driving twice, beat it both times. In Russia, some juvenile stuff. Smuggling, black market, that kind of thing, but very low level. We're talking buying cigarettes in Poland and selling them out of the back of his truck. Then he got started up as a hockey agent over there, and it looks like he was involved in some kind of scandal with a young kid. The kid signed an extension with a Russian club, then left the country and said he signed the contract under duress. Vasily mainly came up in the searches as one of the known associates of a real bad guy. He's the nephew of one Boris Bogdanov."

Tom opened the second folder. It was by far the thickest of the three.

"Boris was born in 1960. Educated at University of Moscow. He speaks Russian, English, German, Polish. After he graduated he went straight into the KGB. Worked in East Germany. Rubbed elbows with none other than current Russian President Vladimir Putin. Boris was a bit of a hatchet man. The Germans suspect, although they cannot prove, that he was involved in the deaths of several prominent dissidents. Writers, scientists, so on. They can't prove it because the official ruling in each case was suicide. By jumping from a high place."

"Holy fucking shit," I said.

Tom smiled.

"Anyway, Boris returned to Russia just before the wall fell and though he was named in some investigations, truth commissions, that sort of thing, none of it stuck. After the fall of communism he was out of work and with Yeltsin in power he was out of fashion. He comes up quite a lot in police reports during this time. Drugs, human trafficking, you name it. But it's all second hand, a guy who knew a guy. No one in his inner circle rolled over on him.

"Of particular note is that in the late nineties Boris was implicated in a rather wide-ranging art scam in Japan. You're familiar with Soviet Realism?"

Dean nodded, but I said: "Nope."

"Well, it's the kind of painting Norman Rockwell would have done under Stalinism. It was a joke for a long time but it came back in vogue after the end of the Cold War. And there was a big scandal when it turned out many of those pictures, particularly those sold in Japan, were forgeries. Our boy Boris's name again comes up. He was mentioned by a disgraced art dealer. But that dealer didn't deal directly with Boris, and the man who acted as the intermediary disappeared. The Russians wouldn't extradite Boris and a lot of the Japanese victims are too embarrassed to testify. Boris skated away again."

I looked at Dean but he was staring at his feet and drumming his fingers on the table.

"In 2000 Putin came to power in Russia," Tom said. "You would think Boris would be back in favour, but nope. He immigrated to Canada almost immediately. He had big money in the bank, I guess, and planned to start a business. After he arrived in Canada there's nothing on him. When I say nothing, I mean nothing. The guy doesn't even have a driver's licence."

Tom closed the folder and put it down, and opened the last one.

"I also did a quick search on your friend Desean," Tom said. "His juvenile record has been expunged, although safe to say he had one considering where he grew up. As an adult he has only been charged once. Human trafficking and living off the avails of prostitution. But he wasn't convicted. It looks like the state was relying on two witnesses. One of them recanted her testimony. And the other one? Guess."

Tom closed the final folder, looked at me and smiled.
"The other," I said, "killed herself by jumping off a bridge."
"You got it," Tom said.
"Can I see the folders?" I asked.
"Be my guest," Tom said.
I opened the one for Boris and paused at the first page.
"What's this photo from?" I asked.
"It's from the eighties," Tom said. "It was the only one in the file."

I stared hard at the picture, trying to remember how I knew that face. The short, light blond hair. The blue eyes. Looked a little like somebody famous, I just couldn't remember who.
And then I knew. I dropped the file like I'd been scalded.
"What?" Dean said. "What?"
"This is the guy," I said.
"What guy?"
"This is the guy from the fishing store!" I said.

40

I jumped up and started pacing back and forth frantically.

"What the fuck man?" I said. "He's seen my face when I went into his store! Now he knows that I was talking to Ha, he's got his fucking adopted son or whatever following me around, they're going to throw me off a bridge …"

"Unlikely," Tom said.

"Unlikely?" I shouted. "That's supposed to make me feel better?"

"Hey," Dean said. "Have you been writing your daily reports?"

"What does that mean?"

"Well," Dean said. "If you have, not much sense in killing you, is there?"

"What?" I asked.

Tom wasn't even paying attention. He'd gone back to writing in his little book.

"There's no point in killing you," Dean said. "Right? Look, what does this guy Boris know about you? You're a private detective and you're sniffing around his business. What's the point of whacking you? If they did, someone else from your agency would just get the file. And they'd read your notes. Right? And then they'd just call the cops."

"Which is what we should do right now," I said.

"Sure," Dean said. "We'll do that soon."

Something about his tone wasn't very reassuring.

"But in the meantime," Dean said, "I don't think you have too much to worry about. I think Desean is trying to learn a bit about you. Maybe even scare you too. Show that they know where you live. That kind of thing. But kill you? No way."

"A picture is starting to emerge," Tom said. "Uncle Boris, at the very least, is a human trafficker and a pimp, and he runs such a smooth operation that there isn't any significant dirt even on his chief lieutenant. This Oksana, or Tanya, is one of his girls. Nephew Vasily is either an associate or a customer or both. Vasily and Oksana make a little extra money through Brucie."

"And this comic thing," Dean said. "It sounds like Uncle Boris's work for sure. Are you kidding me? What easy money. Once you get those fake comics in the box, you've got nothing to worry about. Who is ever going to open them?"

"I don't disagree," Tom said. "But there is no evidence linking Vasily or Boris to the comics, other than that Vasily knew both Derek Ha and Brucie Goldstein. We need that evidence."

"And you don't want the cops to do it, do you?" I asked. "Why would you? You don't want to publicize that CQC got fooled. You want to keep it all on the down low."

"I think we all want the same thing here, Mr. Delacroix," he said.

I wasn't so sure of that, at all.

"Well," Dean said. "Let's be clear here. We can't leave Terrell twisting in the wind for too much longer. On the other hand, Tom's right. All we have right now is a theory. And Boris knows something is up. He's sniffing the wind right now. If we get any closer, I bet you anything he's going to get on a plane disappear, and get rid of anything that could connect him to all this."

"Do you mean Oksana?" I asked.

"Well, come on Terrell," Dean said. "If we talk to the cops, and they talk to Vasily, and then you read about how Oksana jumped off a bridge, how are you going to feel?"

He had a point.

"Still," Tom said. "I don't know how much more evidence you're going to dig up, now that Ha is dead."

"Here's what I'm thinking," Dean said. "We all know Vasily likes to wheel and deal. He makes a lot of money but he spends it as fast as he gets it and he's always broke. That means that he's always on the lookout for a scam. What if I drop a hint about some lawyer wanting some comic books?"

"What?" I said.

Tom leaned back in his chair and tapped his pen thoughtfully on his desk.

"Subtly," Dean continued. "I just say, I know this guy, he's looking for these issues of Batman, or whatever, I found them but they were in poor condition. And then see what he does."

"Can you get me his phone?" Tom said.

"This is fucked up," I announced. No one listened.

"His phone?" Dean asked.

"Sure. You get me his phone and I can make sure we're in on all of his calls. Then you drop your line about the comics, and we see who he calls and who he texts."

"We can even buy the fake comics off him," Dean said. "Then when we go to the police this isn't just speculation. They bust Vasily, he rolls on Boris, boom! No one gets away this time."

"What do you think, Mr. Delacroix?" Tom said. "You going to give us another week?"

"Do I have any choice?" I asked.

"Sure," he said. "We can't stop you from marching down to the police station right now and spilling your guts."

"Don't you think we could get them in on it now?" I asked. "Maybe the cops could help us out."

Tom didn't like that all. To give him credit, Dean considered it.

"The thing is," he said finally, "is that right now, you're their suspect. They don't trust you. We'd have to sell them on it. If we go in there and lay this all on the table, with no evidence, are they really going to team up with us to run a sting? And can we trust them? Are we totally sure that Boris doesn't have any little birds in the TPS? Plus, Aston. I mean, on a certain level, I respect his dedication. But if he pulls the same shit on Boris, or even Vasily, that he did with you, we're fucked. I'm not saying he would do it, mind you. Boris has this big Interpol file and maybe he'd be really careful. But maybe not."

"All right," I said. "We'll try this. But I'm going to the cops after and making a full statement, whether it works or not."

"Nice," Dean said. "I already know Vasily's playing poker this Saturday. We'll do the switch then. Let's do this thing."

41

On Saturday night Tom, Dean and I drove down to Dundas and Spadina in the surveillance van. We parked on a little side street just to the north of Alex Furs. Dean went out to play poker. Tom went into the back of the van to get ready. He had a black briefcase filled with tiny screwdrivers and electronic components neatly organized into little Tupperware containers, and he unpacked it onto a folding table.

My responsibility was to go on a food run to the Vietnamese restaurant next door, a real garish place with neon lighting and clear plastic tables. I ordered us two large servings of pho, one of them with extra tripe and liberal squirtings of Sriracha sauce. That one went to Tom.

"Hoo," Tom said. "Spicy."

"Yeah, it's Vietnamese," I said.

"What's this stuff?" he said, lifting up a tangle of tripe with his fork (he did not use chopsticks). "It looks like a plastic spider web."

"I think it's a kind of noodle," I said.

But the guy was a fucking garburator, and down it all went. I didn't know whether to be disappointed, envious or impressed. Then he leaned back, relaxed and confident, and folded his hands across his stomach, and waited as patiently as a statue.

We only had to wait about thirty minutes before the knock came. I stood up and opened the back door of the van and found myself staring at Oksana's lovely cleavage.

"Hello," she said.

"Uh," I replied.

She held up the Blackberry.

"I hope it won't take long," she said. "He will notice it's gone."

I grabbed it and handed it to Tom, who spared one hard glance for the Russian girl huddling against the cold. Then he got to work. He cracked open the Blackberry in about fifteen seconds and actually soldered a bit of electronics inside it. My mind was blown at how quickly his fingers worked. Then, with a snap, he put it back together and handed it to me.

"The tricky part is he can't turn it on for at least five minutes," he said.

"I will put it back in his jacket," Oksana said, "and he'll turn it on when he turns it on."

She gave me one last glance with those big eyes and then swished away, leaving a little cloud of some dainty fragrance behind her. I closed the door and sat down. Part of me was expecting Tom to make some sort of crack, but he never did, just opened his laptop and started fiddling with it. Having taken care of my two responsibilities (driving and getting dinner) there was nothing for me to do but play some Angry Birds.

About fifteen minutes later Tom said: "He turned it on."

I sat up. A grey, functional software program was running on Tom's nondescript Dell laptop. It looked like a music player crossed with Excel. Tom put on a pair of earphones.

"He's making a call," he said.

"Put it on speaker," I said.

Tom ignored me, so I pranced from one foot to the other like a little kid that needed to go to the bathroom. Finally Tom took the headphones off and turned to me.

"It was all in Russian," he said. "Want me to play it for you?"

"Did you hear any words you recognized?"

"Nope," Tom said. "I don't speak Russian."

So I went back to Angry Birds. I was at this one level that was totally brutal, and the way those pigs snickered at me every time I came up short really pissed me off. I started hitting the replay button really quickly so I didn't need to see it.

Finally there was another tap at the back door. This time it was Dean.

"I think he made the call," Dean said. "Did you get it?"

"Yeah," I said. "But it was in Russian."

"I heard," Dean said. "He jumped on the comic thing like nobody's business. Seemed really eager. After the call he said he would have to work on it but he thought he could help me out."

"Why'd you send the girl?" Tom asked.

"Well, I took the phone, but I didn't have any way to get it to you guys."

"It seems risky," I said.

"Hey," Dean said. "The minute she saw me, she could have thrown me under the bus. Okay? She didn't do it. It was the only way to get the phone out, so I did it."

"Whatever," I said.

"Can you trace that number?" Dean asked.

"I already have," Tom replied. "He called a landline. Looks like a rural address in someplace called Keswick."

"Great," Dean said. "We'll need to get that call translated."

"Already did that too," Tom said. "I e-mailed the audio file to a friend of mine on standby. It was a short call and he sent me back a transcript."

Tom opened up his Gmail and showed it to us. Dean leaned over Tom's shoulder and read it out loud:

"Voice one: Good evening Vanya! How's your health? Voice two: What is this about? Voice one: Nothing, just calling to see how you are doing my friend. Also, I have a little bit of work for you. More comics. Voice two: I don't know what you are talking about. I think you have the wrong number."

Dean straightened back up and shook his head. "Wrong number, holy shit."

"What does that mean?" I asked.

"This fellow Vanya runs a tight ship, is what it means," Dean replied. "No talking on the phone."

"You all want to go out there now?" Tom said, turning around from the computer to look at us.

"You mean right now?" I asked.

Tom raised his eyebrows.

"You don't want to think about it a bit first?" Dean said.

"Well," Tom said. "We know he's at home now. We don't know for how long. I know your boy's anxious to get this over with."

"Don't call me boy," I said.

"No offence intended," he said. "But don't you?"

"Yeah," I said. "Let's do it. Get this son of a bitch out of bed at midnight. Rattle his cage a bit."

"Okay," Dean said. "If that's how you guys want to do it."

42

It took about an hour to get to Keswick. The house was old-fashioned, narrow by modern standards. The lights on the ground floor were all blazing. A long hedge ran around the edge of the property, neat and well maintained, not raggedy at all. Gravel crunched under our wheels as we turned up the driveway.

Dean turned around in his seat to talk to Tom in the back. "So how do we play this?" he asked.

"Well, you should stay here," Tom said. "If he gives your description to Vasily it could blow your cover."

"Yeah," Dean said. "But I've got an idea. Let's all go."

"Okay," Tom said.

Before we knocked on the front door, Tom had us circle around the house, carefully stepping over the plants in the gardens. At one window, around the back, Tom froze in place and Dean started to laugh.

"Bingo," Dean said.

"What?" I whispered.

The room was a recent addition, a solarium, with big windows. The sofas looked very old and broken in, and there was a little coffee table and a small bookshelf. A large oil painting dominated the rear wall. It was of soldiers sitting and standing in a circle during the winter, many of them wearing fur hats and long coats.

"A little ballsy isn't it?" Dean said.

"That's why he's got it in the back," Tom said. "And anyway, who's going to recognize it?"

"What is it?" I said.

"It's called 'Rest After the Battle'," Dean said, "and it's one of the most famous paintings to come out of Stalinist Russia."

We walked back to the front of the house and Tom knocked on the door. Footsteps approached from the other side.

"Who is it?" a voice called in accented English.

"Police," Tom said. "Open up."

"Do you have a warrant?" the voice said. "Put the warrant through the mail slot."

Unperturbed, Tom took a piece of paper out of his jacket, folded it twice and slid it through the mail slot. Then he waited a moment before suddenly and viciously kicking the front door, right beneath the knob. It had been chained and bolted, but the door itself was old and thin, like the walls of the little farmhouse, and the wood snapped and splintered. The old man Vanya, who had been crouching to retrieve the 'warrant', was bowled over.

"Holy shit!" I said.

Tom stormed inside like a Marine in Basra. "Gun!" he cried, and a moment later a small metal object flew out the door and skittled to a stop at my feet. It was a Glock.

"Augh!" Vanya shouted. "Don't! Don't!"

Tom hauled the old man to his feet and twisted his arm behind his back.

"Easy," Dean said.

"Got any more surprises for us?" Tom said. "Got anything else?"

"You're breaking it! You're breaking my arm!"

"Answer the question."

"No, no!"

Tom frog-marched Vanya back into the house.

"Jesus," Dean muttered, and followed, carefully stepping around the gun. I followed.

When I came into the solarium, Vanya was sitting in a leather Lay-Z-Boy cradling his arm. He had a scraggly white beard and big, soulful eyes, like a little kid. Tom was looming over him. Dean had gone off somewhere.

"Nice painting," Tom said. "Where'd you get it?"

Vanya didn't say anything. In the silence I could hear Dean moving around the house.

"I asked you a question," Tom said. "Where'd you get this painting?"

"Who are you?" Vanya asked. "You are not police."

Tom leaned forward and looked right into Vanya's eyes and said: "You're right. I'm not police. I'm here on behalf of someone you ripped off. Do you understand that?"

Vanya looked like he understood, all right. He swallowed and shrank back from Tom.

"Hey," Dean called from somewhere. "Found his studio."

"Come on," Tom said. "Come with me."

We walked through the kitchen and then trooped down the stairs to the basement. The ceiling was low and the floor was bare but it was clean, and extremely well lit by fluorescent lighting.

Unfinished paintings hung on the walls. Most, but not all, were very abstract. One even I recognized.

"Is that Marilyn Monroe?" I asked.

"Andy Warhol's very hot these days," Dean said. "Not exactly the trickiest thing to forge either. Are these supposed to be Damien Hirst dot paintings?"

Vanya was staring at the floor.

"Interesting hobby, you've got here," Dean said.

"Who is your client?" Vanya asked.

"Who is yours?" Dean replied.

Vanya laughed.

Dean kept walking around the room until he came to a desk in the corner. "Now this is what we're really interested in."

A big fancy case of pencil crayons stood on the desk, with every color of the rainbow, and every one in between. Next to it were rolls of tape, different boxes of staples, liquids in plastic squeeze bottles, a small metal press and what looked like a little specialized iron. Box-cutters hung from hooks on the back wall.

And in the drawers Dean found a bunch of old comics that had clearly been worked on. They were missing pages, or they'd been trimmed, or parts of them had been colored or drawn on.

When Dean held them in his hands, I do have to admit that I felt a little thrill of satisfaction. There it was. Proof. Vasily had been involved in restoring comic books.

"Looks like you've got a sweet little set up here," Dean said.

"You came for comics?" Vanya said. He sounded disgusted.

"Not much of a fan, are you?" Dean asked.

"I cannot believe you break in my door and threaten me in my home over comics."

"You defrauded people of tens of thousands of dollars. Maybe hundreds."

"Bah," Vanya said. "The forger is not like the plagiarist. A plagiarist, he takes credit for the work of someone else. This is a great crime. The forger does the reverse. He makes something and he gives credit for it to someone else. This is a crime that only harms fools with too much money. What does it matter who makes the thing if the buyer cannot tell the difference? Did he not get what he paid for? He wanted a picture of dots, now he has picture of dots. You know the hardest part of forging the works of Hirst is not the paintings, but the certificate of authenticity. It has a hologram. Painting dots is easy."

Dean smiled.

"That's one way of looking at it," he said.

"And the comics?" Vanya said. "This is not even forgery. It is restoration. Before I came to this country, I worked in cathedrals that had been destroyed by the Nazis in the Great Patriotic War, and stood neglected for years under the godless communists. Who are these idiot Americans to say I cannot do for a cheap children's book why I did for great works of art?"

"Well," Dean said, "you knew what the market was and you lied to people. When the fraud comes out, hundreds of thousands of dollars will be wiped out. And if you trace those dollars back to see where they went, it's ultimately in your pockets."

"Why must the fraud come out?" Vanya said. "Where is the crime if the comics stay in their little boxes? We are like alchemists. We turn lead into gold. It is you who are changing it back. And for what? Keep the boxes closed. Everyone will be happy."

"Right. If no one actually examines the underlying value of the item in question, its value will never go down. You should have worked for a bond-rating agency. You'd have made more money and you'd only have to worry about the OSC, not the police."

Vanya didn't have anything to say to that.

"Think about your situation," Dean said. "We have a good idea who you work for. And he's pretty hardcore. No doubt about it. So keeping that in mind, what's he going to do if you pick up the phone and call him and tell him about this? Is he going to show up at my nice house on Bloor West and kill me? Me? A fancy downtown lawyer with a family, who has been keeping detailed notes on my investigation? Or is he going to come over here and throw you off your roof? You tell me what's going to make him safer."

Vanya didn't have anything to say to that either.

"Let's not kid ourselves here," Dean said. "You're in trouble. So why don't you just tell me the story. You don't have to mention any names for now, if it makes you feel better."

For a long time, Vanya didn't say anything. I wasn't sure he would crack. But eventually, he started to speak.

"There are two men. One is old and dangerous. The other is young and a fool. Eight years ago the old one hears of the money in comics. It seems almost too easy. Hundreds of thousands of dollars for tiny restorations. But to sell the comics they must be put in a box by men in Florida. And to get the comics to the men in Florida, they must be sent by a store. And how do we explain to the store where we found so many comics in such good condition? This is where the young fool comes in. He has a friend with a store that helps us. Many comics go into the boxes, we make much money, but eventually the men in Florida start to catch my work. The friend with the store becomes nervous. We lose leverage over him. It's all over. Until this summer."

"Go on," Dean said.

"The old one calls me in July," Vanya continued. "He asks me if I have been talking about the thing with the comics. He asks me if I have been trying to do something on my own. I am very afraid. I tell him that I have said nothing. I ask him if I can expect a visit from the police. He says, no, not the police. He says someone knows and someone is trying to take money from the friend with the store. He says it is no problem. He will take care of it. But he wants to know how it is that people are talking about his business. The old man does not like that. Not at all. I told him I don't know, and I hope with all my heart he believes me. I don't hear from him about this again. That is all."

Dean looked at me, and then at Tom, before turning back to Vanya.

"Okay," Dean said. "That's it."

"That's it?" Vanya asked.

"Just this. If they get in touch with you about some more work, then do it. That's all. Afterwards the cops might show up. At that point, call me, and we'll hook you up with a serious lawyer."

Dean handed Vanya a card.

"Dean, are you sure you want to do that?" I said.

"Well," Dean replied. "You just said my name."

Shit, I thought.

I could feel Tom smirking at me.

"We both know," Dean said to Vanya, "that you can't be safe while the old man is out there. You know too much. Call me, and we'll make sure you get protection. We'll also make sure the old man can't hurt you anymore."

Vanya looked at the card, but said nothing more.

Once we were outside, Tom said:

"Well, you sure stuck your neck out."

"He'll go for it," Dean said. "Of course he will."

"If you say so," Tom said.

43

Monday was the day of my big meeting with Mrs. Burke. So I dragged my fat ass out of bed, showered, put on my best suit with my lucky monkey tie. At the subway station I picked up a huge coffee and a Cinnabon, with pecans. By the time she arrived, I felt ready to go.

Mrs. Burke sat down across the desk from me. She was wearing a pink hooded Lululemon track suit and her hair was pulled back in a severe ponytail. A 100% humorless expression was on her face. Grim, I'd describe it. Like someone who was fighting a hard battle with all her strength but losing a little bit every day.

"Thanks for coming in, Mrs. Burke."
"What is this all about?" she said. "Did you find anything?"
"The investigation is still ongoing."
"Well that what have you got to say?" she said, her voice rising. "Are you trying to talk me out of it? After I've …"

"Mrs. Burke," I said, interrupting her. "You're a very strong-willed individual. What that means is that we haven't had some of the basic conversations with you that we would normally have with anyone in your situation. Now I don't feel right about that. And so even though I know you don't like it and you don't want to hear it, we're going to have a chat about what your goals are. Okay? No one's billing you for this time."

"You think this is about money?" she said. "God! What's so hard for you men to understand? It's such a double standard. 'Oh, so your husband is playing around a little. Don't worry! That's just guy stuff! He still loves you baby!' Do you really say that kind of thing to men that come in here about their wives? Is that what you'd have me believe?"

"As a matter of fact," I said, "we do. Most people don't listen, whether they're men or women. But it's important to have the conversation up front. Do you know why?"

She glared at me without saying anything.

"Because when people do find out, they're usually unhappy. Many of them wish they didn't know. They've paid us hundreds, in some case thousands, of dollars, and they wish they could all take it back. Men and women. That's just a fact."

"Fine, you've said your piece."

"But," I continued, "we aren't talking about most people, or our other clients. We're talking about you and your particular situation." I looked down at my hands. To tell you the truth, for all my talk about how this was a standard conversation, I really didn't have much idea what I was going to say. "And it's just, Mrs. Burke, it seems to me that you should just ask yourself how much you really want to know. That's all."

"So I shouldn't want to know if my husband's cheating on me?"

"Well," I said, "we can never prove a negative. We can look and look but we can never conclusively prove that he isn't cheating on you, right?"

"He is doing it," she said. "I know."

"How?"

"I can tell."

"How, though?"

"A million little things," she snapped. "The way he drinks his coffee in the morning! The inflection of his voice when he says he's going out on business! The fact that he," and here she started weeping, "he doesn't touch me the same way anymore! I know! All right? I know."

"So," I said, "then just leave him. Get a divorce. You don't need proof of adultery to do that."

"No, I have to be sure," she said. "I have to really know."

I think she recognized the irrationality of what she was saying, but I didn't point it out directly.

"But I told you," I said. "We can never conclusively prove your husband didn't cheat on you. So unless we catch him in the act, we'll never know."

"You will if you do your job," she shrieked. "Because I know he's cheating on me!"

I wondered what Mr. Burke would do if he could see his wife now, her face all puffy from suffering, her eyes red from crying. Was he used to it? Or did it cut him up inside? Or both?

"God," she said, wiping her eyes. "I don't even know what we're talking about any more."

"We're talking about what you want," I said. "A suspicion has taken hold in your mind. It could be right, or it could be wrong. We can't prove it wrong, to make it go away. You have to ask yourself: so what if it is right? What does it change? Do I need to know? Really? Or can you accept not knowing? Can I accept that, and just live with this man? Do I really need to pry open this box? What's in there that I really want to find?"

She was starting to get herself together. It looked like she knew that answering my questions hadn't gone so well so she didn't respond to my point.

"My mind is made up, Mr. Delacroix. Now do you want to keep working on this file or not?"

"Are you sure?" I asked. "Really sure? I won't do this again; this is your last chance. Do you want to take a day to think things over?"

"No!" she said. "Now do you want to keep working on this file or not?"

"There's no need," I said. "I already caught him."

For someone who claimed to have been so sure, she sure looked awfully surprised. Stricken, you might even say.

I pushed a file folder across the table to her but she didn't move to open it. She just looked at me.

"It's all in the file," I said. "He was having an affair with Anna Herowicz, a young artist who had a show at his studio. And he was meeting with her in the mornings, in the park near your house, when he was going out for his run. The pictures are in there."

But her hands stayed in her lap and she didn't look at the folder, or at me. She opened her mouth to say something, but no words came out. Instead her lower lip started to shake and her face bunched up and she leaned her head on my desk and started to cry.

When she left, she didn't take the folder. I put it aside for her but she never ended up coming to pick it up.

Everybody went for lunch at the Unicorn; Alan was equal parts elated and disgusted.

"You couldn't have milked it just a little fucking longer, Hercule fucking Poirot?" he shouted at me after everyone in the office had pounded back an Irish Car Bomb (it was a special occasion). "You had to kill the fucking goose that laid the golden eggs? This guy's like, fuck the firm, I'm a master detective, and this is how I roll. Well fuck you, Terrell Delacroix, you magnificent bastard. Fuck you right in your whorish mouth."

And then he raised his glass, and I did, and everyone was laughing, even me, but part of me felt like crying.

I did cry a little later that night. I had this weird feeling that things couldn't go on like this, like something would have to give, but I didn't know what.

44

The next day Alan gave me some more work. To my relief, they were all simple personal injury files.

Around four pm I got a call from Dean.

"Hey Terrell," he said. "How are you doing?"

"A little off my game today," I said. "How about you?"

"Okay, but here's the thing. I just got a call from Vasily."

"Yes?" I said. "Did he get the stuff?"

"Well, he says he did."

"Great!" I said. "And that means this shit is over, right?"

"Yep," he said. "One way or another it ends tonight."

"What's the plan?" I asked.

"He wants to meet me up at a restaurant he owns at Yonge and Sheppard," Dean said. "He wants me to be there at eleven pm."

I got a bit nervous about this.

"Can't you meet somewhere else?" I asked.

"Why?"

"Well, what if Vanya rolled on us?" I said. "What if it's a trap?"

"I don't think so dude," he said. "Anyway, you and Tom can wait in the car outside."

"Should we call the cops?"

"Oh come on, Terrell. And risk them blowing it? When we're this close? Look man, if I don't come back, you just go ahead and avenge my death. All right?"

I had to hand it to Dean. It had pissed me off when I thought he didn't care about my safety, but he was just as cavalier when it was his ass on a line. So I told him sure, he could play it however he wanted to, if we were closing down the file tomorrow.

The restaurant was a little Greek place in a shopping plaza between a Laundromat and a convenience store. Dean went in at 10:45 while Tom and I waited in the white panel van in the parking lot, around the side of the building. Tom had fixed Dean up with a camera and a microphone and now he was sitting with his computer in his lap, listening through big earphones and staring at the grainy image on the screen. I was dicking around with my iPhone, feeling useless, and also hungry, despite that I'd had a twelve inch pulled pork sub for dinner.

"Anything yet?" I'd ask Tom every five minutes, and he'd smile at me and not answer.

The time ticked by until 11:30, enough time for me to get really nervous. Tom lifted up his hands to his headset and frowned. Then he looked at me.

"He's coming out," he said.

And indeed after a few seconds someone knocked at the door. We opened it.

"I just got a call from Vasily," Dean said. "He's had some car trouble and he's parked on Sheppard just west of here. Right on the bridge over the West Don River and Earl Bales Park."

"The bridge?" I said. "Oh, no man. That's fucked up."

"It's a public place," Dean said.

"But it's exposed," Tom said. "You'll have to go alone."

"Well, what do we do?" Dean said.

"I'll drive by first," Tom said. "Check it out, offer to help him out. If he doesn't take it, I'll park the car on the other side, head back on foot, set up somewhere underneath the bridge."

Tom motioned to the black duffel bag he'd brought with him.

"I've got some things in here," he said. "A night vision scope. I can keep an eye on things from down below."

"Okay," Dean said.

"I'm going with you," I said.

"No way," Dean said.

"Yes," I said. "I'm fucking going. You're not leaving me behind. I'll sit in the back. But someone's got to be there in case they try to throw you off, and try to make it look like just a lonely man taking a jump cause he's been fighting with his wife."

"He's right," Tom said, which surprised me a bit.

Dean looked at me and grinned.

"My man," he said.

"We shouldn't be doing this at all," I said.

"Come on, come on," Dean said. "We're almost done."

45

Tom drove off in the van and I slouched down the backseat of Dean's car.

"Seriously, this is fucked up," I said.

"Hmm," Dean said, as he drummed his fingers on the wheel. Then he said: "Funny you should mention my marital difficulties. Tina went back to California yesterday, took both the kids."

"Fuck."

"She said I was welcome to come down with her if I wanted to try to sort things out," Dean said. "I'm still licensed to practice law in California."

"I'm sorry," I said.

"Don't worry about it," Dean replied. "There's going to be plenty of time to figure everything out soon."

We waited for a while.

"Dean," I said. "Do you remember that story you told me? About the guy who thought he could taste the chemicals in McDonalds coffee?"

"Yeah," he said.

"And you just let him go on believing it?"

"Yeah."

"Do you ever wish you could do that to yourself? Just let yourself keep believing a lie?"

He didn't say anything for a while. I was worried he was pissed at me. When he spoke, his voice was very, very small.

"Sometimes," he whispered. "Sometimes."

A minute later his phone buzzed and he picked it up.

"Yeah. Yeah. Okay. We'll give you another couple of minutes and then we'll head down."

Dean put the phone down.

"Vasily's parked on the south side, the eastbound side of the bridge with the hood of his car popped up. Tom asked if he needed any help but Vasily said his friend was coming to pick him up. Now Tom's heading down into the park, said he just needs a few minutes to get ready."

"Okay," I said. "Dean, do you ever think that maybe, I mean, it's kind of what's cool about you, that skepticism, but maybe in the long run …"

"Terrell," he said. "Here is the fact of the matter. You can't go back. Okay? Once that doubt sets in, then you have to know. There's no turning back. Once you get that doubt. And I get it all the time. What can you do? That's life."

Dean started the car. We drove west on Sheppard. Eventually we came to the bridge, crossing over yet another one of the ravines that dissected the city.

I couldn't see where we were going because I was crouched down behind the seats, but I felt the car pull over onto the left hand side of the road and then roll to a halt.

"Here goes nothing," Dean muttered, and he stepped out of the car. I heard him say: "Hey man! What's up?"

And then there was silence. No matter how hard I strained, I couldn't hear anything, until the tap at the window. I looked over to my right and saw Vasily staring right at me. He had a gun, and he was motioning for me to get out of the car.

46

Once I was standing next to Dean at the edge of the bridge, Vasily popped the hood of our car. Meaning that we were standing between two parked cars, both with their hoods popped, so we were sheltered from prying eyes from both directions. Boris and Vasily stood facing us with their backs to the road. To anyone driving by, we just looked like two vehicles stopped for a quick jump start.

I had never been so frightened in my life. I was literally shaking under my jacket.

Dean, on the other hand, looked locked in, and he never took his eyes of Boris's face.

When Boris spoke, I was struck again by his lack of an accent.

"Where'd your friend go?" he asked. "The technician?"

And then we heard it drift across the air to us, sounding more like a pop than a bang really: gunfire.

Boris allowed himself the briefest of smiles.

"There," he said softly.

And suddenly I knew we were going to die. He wasn't going to stand here and explain his evil plot. He wasn't going to put us in some elaborate death trap and then walk out of the room. He was just going to shoot us. This was the end. This was it.

And then Dean spoke:

"Want to know where the money went, Boris?"

Boris said nothing, but he didn't shoot us either.

"Brucie didn't have it. The day he died, he called up his cleaning lady in a panic asking about a missing black box. What was in the box? The money of course. Where did it go? Someone took it, right? Who? But then, what do you care? It wasn't yours. Two-hundred-and-fifty grand is a lot of money, but so what, right?"

At the mention of the number, Vasily jerked in surprise. Boris said nothing. Every now and then a car would pass behind them and I would consider bolting, or screaming for help, but Boris's gun was trained right on my chest and I didn't move.

"Let me tell you what you really wanted to know: how Brucie found out about the restored comics. Am I right?"

"Are you stalling?" Boris said. "Men like you are always too clever to just beg."

"And you still don't know how he found out," Dean said. "Or else you'd have shot us by now."

"So you're bargaining," Boris said.

Vasily said something nervous to Boris in Russian.

"So who told? Well, someone who knew about the comics, obviously. And someone who was short some cash this summer because of, say, a poker debt. Someone who'd met Brucie because they had a similar taste in women."

And after this last sentence, Boris looked at Vasily carefully, out of the corner of his eye. You could tell that the final piece of the puzzle had just clicked together for him.

Vasily said something urgent in Russian.

Dean looked at Vasily and snarled.

"What do you mean, baa baa baa? Comrade Wolf knows who he is going to eat."

Vasily's eyes were as wide as dinner plates. He shifted back and forth on his feet a couple of times, and then he suddenly raised his gun at Boris. But Boris was faster. He turned and fired in one quick, efficient motion, so quick that he'd almost turned back to us before Vasily hit the ground. But I was jacked up with adrenaline and it was like time was slowing down. I bowled straight into Boris, all two hundred forty pounds of me, and I knocked him over and ended up on top. I tried to hold onto his gun arm but he twisted loose and smacked me with the barrel of the pistol.

And let me tell you: that fucks you up. It's not like the movies where the hero holds his head for a moment, grunts, and then gets back up and keeps fighting. I mean, I felt something snap in my head and there were all these lights and sparks and the whole world turned fuzzy.

But then Dean was on Boris, and they were fighting like mad, and the gun went off a couple of times. Dean cried out and the gun bounced across the pavement. A moment later I heard footsteps banging out a hasty retreat, and then another bang, this one from far away. Boris shouted, not in pain, but frustration. He hit the ground, cursed once in Russian and then he was silent.

Dean was over top of me.
"Terrell, hey, you okay?"
"I don't know man," I said. "I feel funny."
"Just wait," Dean said. "I'm calling 9-1-1. Just hold on a bit. Okay? Just wait."
I was blinking blood out of my eyes, lying on my back.
"What about Boris?"
"He's dead. They're both dead. Just relax. You saved my life. It's going to be all right."

The pain rippled through my head. I wanted to cry but I thought it would hurt too much. And so I just gently whimpered, and Dean held my hand, until the ambulances arrived.

47

So I had a fractured skull. Fractured skulls are bad news, apparently, you can go blind or into a coma or have all sorts of weird problems. In particular, although it was a linear fracture, they were worried about how close it was to a suture. I spent over a week in Sunnydale.

The support I got from the people at work and all of my friends was overwhelming. I couldn't have many visitors but all of the flowers and stuffed animals were piled up around me. Even my ex-wife showed up. I also got a private room and a TV (paid for by Mr. Goldstein, I was told). It made me feel pretty grateful for the relationships I had, a lot less lonely. Something like that really put all my whiny bullshit in perspective.

Dean was there basically all the time. He wasn't always in the room with me, but he was always just down the hall. We didn't talk much, especially at first, when I had such a splitting headache and trouble thinking straight. Other visitors were always coming in and out, and he generally let them do the talking, or headed out for a coffee to leave me alone.

"I'm sorry," he finally said to me.

"Well, I was right," I said. "Your plan was stupid."

"No, you don't understand. I didn't mean you getting hurt. I'm sorry that when you were unconscious, I put my dick on your cheek and took a picture."

I snickered, which made my head hurt.

"Shut the fuck up, it hurts to laugh."

"Sorry," Dean said. He ran his hands through his hair. A dark haze of stubble covered his chin and his eyes looked a little red. "Man. What a fuck-up."

"I'll be fine," I said.

"Yeah, looks that way," Dean said. "But when they got you on the drugs here, you were acting as loopy as shit. I asked the head neurologist when you were going to get better, and he was all like: 'It's impossible to tell. Possibly never.' So I was totally depressed. The next day you seemed better and I asked the nurse and she said: 'Oh, usually we see a big improvement in 48 hours, but we'll have to see.' What a difference those two diagnoses make."

"Doctors are dicks," I said.

"Yeah," Dean said.

After a pause, I said:

"How do you think they figured out what we were up to?"

"Vanya must have told them. I really misjudged him. I'm sorry Terrell."

"Vasily could have figured it out too."

"Yeah, it's possible."

"So what happened on the bridge? Who shot who?"

"Well," Dean said. "Boris shot Vasily."

"I remember that."

"Then we wrestled around with Boris. Eventually he tried to make a run for it, but someone shot him with a high-powered rifle."

"Tom?"

"Undoubtedly. But he's gone. Back to Florida I guess, or wherever. Cops are looking for him but I don't think they'll have much luck. They searched the park and found Desean's body, shot through the head, holding a gun that had apparently been fired once."

"I guess he missed."

"Yep," Dean said. "That must have been the shot we heard."

"So that's that," I said.

"Anyway, just so you know, I made a full statement to the cops."

"Really?"

"Yeah," Dean said.

"Like, full full?" I asked.

He smiled a little.

"I left out anything about Oksana," he said.

"How did you do that?"

"You know that stripper you chatted up at the Rail? I told them that she told you she'd seen Vasily and Brucie together."

"You slick son of a bitch," I said.

"Well, you tell them whatever you want when you talk to them," he said. "I'm not asking you to lie."

"I was wondering why I hadn't seen them yet."

"I sort of cut a deal with Angry Detective Unabrow. He was hitting the roof, as you can imagine, but I basically said, I'm going to lay everything out honestly for you, and in return, let Terrell recoup till he gets out of the hospital. The gloomy head neurologist came in handy there. Probably he told Aston something like: 'You can question him if you like, but I can't promise it won't instantly kill him.'"

"Ha," I said.

"Anyway, they're up to their asses in alligators," Dean said. "Aston was skeptical at first, or at least he pretended to be. But when they got a confirmation on Boris's ID shit got real. Plus someone in the police department leaked part of the story and it was all over the papers."

"Are we in trouble?" I asked.

"We'll see," Dean said. "Obviously, they're a bit cranky about our amateur detective work. With the benefit of hindsight, maybe they're right."

"You think?" I said.

"My guess is they don't want to make a stink out of anything. The bottom line is it looks like a young man had been killed and they hadn't figured it out, that Boris had been living in the country for years with no one keeping tabs on him, and all the rest of it. They don't want all that in the papers."

"Nice," I said. "Way better than California."

Dean smiled.

"Can you tell me something?" I asked.

"Sure."

"How much of how you handled this was about Oksana?"

Dean looked away. His smile curdled in that particular way of his, and then without looking back at me he said: "All of it, Terrell. It was all for her."

"You're crazy," I said.

"More than you know," he replied.

48

A couple of days after I got out of the hospital, while I was still hanging around my apartment watching Breaking Bad on DVD and not doing too much, I got a call from Dean. He was going over to Jay Goldstein's place to have one last chat about the whole situation and he wanted me to come with him. I told him fine, that I'd walk over and meet him there.

I walked to Jay's house and rang the doorbell. It took a while for anyone to answer. Eventually I heard Jay's slow footsteps and the door opened.

"There he is," Jay said. "Good to see you up on your feet again."

The clothes Jay was wearing looked too big for him, his face was worn, his hair was thinner and grey. When he smiled it looked like something was going to crack.

"I heard you hooked me up at the hospital," I said. "Thanks a lot. I really owe you big time."

"It was the least I could do," Jay said. "I'm very sorry about what happened to you. Come on in."

Dean hadn't arrived yet so we went back to the solarium together and each had a fancy beer. I wasn't sure what to talk about after the usual pleasantries. So I finally said:

"How's your legal situation going?" I asked. "If you don't mind me asking."

"Oh, it's going," Jay said.

"What's happening next?"

"Looks like my lawyer is going to bring a preliminary motion trying to strike the notice of allegations," he said. "Which is interesting, because you don't see that too often in these sorts of proceedings. He thinks we can knock it out."

"Dean explained it to me," I said. "It sounds like bullshit."

"Well, that's certainly my position," Jay said.

"How are things going at the firm?" I asked, trying to change the subject.

"Didn't Dean tell you?"

Shit, I thought.

"No," I said.

"Well, it's tough to keep doing what I do until this is sorted out, for any number of reasons, and it looks like it might be a long time until it does get sorted out. If the motion I was talking about gets appealed, for instance, it could take years even before that gets finished. So it looks like I'm leaving the firm."

"Oh," I said.

"Yes," Jay said. "I'm just working on transitioning everything."

"Are you going be okay?" I asked.

"Money isn't a problem," he said. "I just don't know what I'm going to do with myself."

"Well, I'm sorry to hear that," I said.

Jay shrugged.

"Just one of those things," he said.

The doorbell rang and Jay shuffled to the front door, like an old man, and then returned with Dean. Dean bumped fists with me and then sat down.

"Well," Dean said. "There's not much left to talk about. Let's just listen to this."

Dean took out his laptop and set it up on a coffee table. After a few minutes he started playing an audio file.

"What's this?" I asked.

A moment later, I heard a voice speaking.

"I still can't believe I'm free."

It was Oksana.

I looked at Dean, questioningly, but he was looking at the computer with one hand over his mouth.

"It will probably take a while to sink in."

The second voice was Dean.

I looked at Jay, but he had no more idea what was going on than I did.

"With a man like Boris, you never think you will be free of him. He was too clever and too cruel. I owe you everything."

There was a rustling noise, like cloth sliding on cloth, and the sound of wood creaking. The recording was made in bed. A little pulse of some unpleasant feeling hit me, like I'd been flashed by an exhibitionist in a trench coat. I didn't want to hear this shit.

"Well, we couldn't have figured it out without you. You were very brave."

"Yes. I was very brave. I am a brave girl for you."

A wet, physical sounding noise.

"What is this?" Jay asked.

Dean said nothing, but his voice spoke from the laptop.

"There's still some things I don't understand though."

"You will never understand everything in life. You should not try."

"Maybe not."

And then the silence spilled out, and there was more movement, and I wondered if that was it, and if so, what was the point, when Dean's voice came again.

"But sometimes you can't help wondering, even if you don't want to."

"Hmm?"

"Like, for example, who exactly killed Brucie?"

"Boris, I thought."

"Well, then why didn't he know how Brucie knew about the restored comics? Because if he and Desean got their hands on Brucie, they would have scared it out of him. But when I talked to Boris on the bridge, he didn't know."

"I don't know. Maybe Vasily killed him."

"Yeah. That makes more sense actually. The night Brucie died, he got a bunch of calls from one number, and then one call from another number. Maybe the first calls were from Boris, and the other number was Vasily asking him to come out of the house. If he did, then maybe Vasily took the money and killed Brucie to cover his tracks."

"Yes, maybe."

"But the money had already been stolen by the time Brucie left the house. How did Vasily get inside Brucie's house to take the

money anyway? Did he have the code to the security system? And a key? And why would Brucie come out of the house if Vasily had already stolen the money?"

"I don't know. What does it matter?"

"You know when I was on the bridge, I mentioned the amount of money Brucie got from Mr. Ha. Two-hundred and fifty-thousand. Vasily's face jerked when I said the number. It was like he was surprised. But why would he be surprised if he was the one who ended up with the money?"

"Oh my god," I said, and looked at Dean, but he was just staring at his computer, his hand covering the bottom of his mouth.

There was nothing but silence for a moment. Finally Dean's voice came on again:

"He babbled on about comics didn't he? Sure he did. A kid like Brucie couldn't think of anything better to talk about with a beautiful woman. And so you and Vasily had an idea. Brucie would hit up jumpy old Mr. Ha for a quick score, and then you would liberate the money from him. And since you were the one entrusted with getting the money from Brucie, you had an opportunity to skim off the top. So you told Vasily you were asking for one number and then got Brucie to demand the two-fifty. Brucie picked up the money, you stole it from him, passed on some of it to Vasily, and kept the rest. Nice plan. Only things went wrong."

"Silence.

"Before the blackmail job, Mr. Ha went to Boris. And Boris, well, if someone is up in his shit he wants to know who, and how. So he bugged the money. You found the bug and left it in Brucie's house, but you still had all sorts of problems. One, you and Vasily spilled the beans about Boris's scheme to a kid, two, you ripped off Derek Ha, three, you'd already been skimming money off this kid for months, four, you'd even ripped off Vasily during the blackmail scam. Now that's a terrible situation."

"I want you to go away." Oksana sounded as if the idea had just occurred to her.

"So Brucie hides in his house. The money is missing. Boris is calling him, or Desean, or both, over and over. He has no one to turn to. But then someone else calls him and he leaves the house. Now who would he do that for?"

"You're sick, you're crazy. You think I killed Brucie? How could I throw him off a bridge?"

"Well, the evidence was never consistent with Brucie being thrown off that bridge anyway. Brucie's fingerprints were upside-down, like he was hanging off the other side. Now why would he do that? Who knows? Here's one theory. Maybe you called him and told him you were afraid of what Boris was going to do to you. Maybe you said you were going to kill yourself. Maybe he rushed out there to find you clinging to one of those pillars, just out of reach from the sidewalk. Maybe he hopped over the railing and tried to help you. Maybe he even reached out his hand. He was a big guy, and not very graceful. All it would have taken was one little tug."

"You are crazy! What proof do you have? That Vasily looked surprised when you said a number? Get out of my house."

"Yeah, it's just a theory. But Detective Aston did pull all the fingerprints off the bridge. They're still in evidence. So unless you were wearing gloves in August, I guess we'll see."

I could hear Oksana gasp, even over the shitty laptop speakers.

"Is that what you come over here to do? To sleep with me and then accuse me of things?"

"No. I came over to look for something. And I found it in a hidden compartment under the sink in the bathroom. I guess the money could have come from anywhere. But if you were going to make that argument, you should have taken it out of the black box you stole it in."

And now Oksana started to cry.

"I loved you. I loved you from the minute I saw you. And you betrayed me like this. You came into my home and betrayed me. I don't think you are capable of loving anyone."

After a long pause, Dean finally said:

"I'm sorry, I can't help myself. Why did Boris call Tom 'the technician'?"

Another moment of silence.

"Boris and Vasily were going to kill us on the bridge because they knew we were trying to set them up. Now there are all sorts of ways they could have figured out what we were up to. But why did *he say, where's your friend the technician? I mean, none of them saw Tom doing anything in the least bit technical. Now who did see something like that, Oksana? Who saw something like that?"*

She didn't answer, and so the last words on the recording belonged to Dean.

"What are you thinking when you look at me like that?"
A beat went by.
"The thing is, no matter what you say, I'll never really know."
Dean pressed a button on the laptop, and it stopped.

We both looked at Jay. Jay had this look on his face fit to fucking break your heart. Like he was seeing everything around him without seeing it, do you know what I mean? Like that big brain of his was racing as fast as it could to think of something to say, but say what?

"I see," he said. And then, in a very small voice: "I wonder why I ever thought any of this would make me feel any better."
I looked down at my feet.
"I wonder," Jay said.
"I already went to the cops," Dean said. "I took the money, I gave them the recording. I did that all yesterday. So everything's done and over with."
"That's good," Jay said.

Jay's eyes roved around the room, as if they were trying to find something they could rest on for a little while, but weren't having any luck.
Dean stood up.
"I'll swing by in a couple of days," Dean said. "Before you head out east to meet Janet."
"All right," Jay said. "I'd like that."
They shook hands.
"Dean," Jay said. "What I said there, I didn't mean it. I appreciate what you did. I know what you gave up for this."
"I know," Dean said. "It's all right."

"I still have a lot of friends in this city and if you decide to stay in Toronto I can still help you."

"Thanks," Dean said. "That means a lot to me. Thanks."

Then Jay shook my hand, slowly.

"Nice to meet you, Terrell," he said. "I appreciate all your hard work."

"No problem sir," I said.

"I hope you feel better soon."

"Thank you."

And then he ushered us out.

A moment after the door shut, Dean looked at me.

"Let's get drunk," he said.

My stomach balled up. I wanted to say: it's your life, but just think about it for 24 hours. Just take that and ice it, table it, stash it away. The booze will still be there tomorrow if you want it. But man, the hurt on his face. The naked pain. And those silences playing on the laptop, the sound of Dean's voice (*no matter what you say, I'll never really know*).

I didn't have the heart.

"All right," I said. "Fuck it."

49

We ended up at this high-end sushi place in Yorkville. On a weekday, at three pm, the place was deserted. We sat right up at the bar, eating edamame and wasabi beans and pounding sake bombs. The chef kept smiling and nodding at us, like he remembered us from somewhere and wanted to come up and say hi, but was too busy.

It's a lot of fun to watch those guys work up close. Everything he needed was right in front of him in separate little containers. Nothing ever spilled. He did most of the work with his sharp knife, which he regularly dipped in water. Smoked eel, raw salmon and tuna, rice, seaweed, roe. The tips of his fingers were wet and he shaped everything with practiced, effortless motions. Nothing stuck to him.

One platter after another appeared in front of us, and we attacked it like it was a race. Or more precisely, I attacked it like it was a race, a race in which I was intent on lapping my opponent, numerous times if possible.

We started out laughing our heads off, mostly about stuff from back in California. Parties we went to, the stupid shit the idiots we worked with used to do, the trip we took to Vegas and Arizona together. But after a while it dawned on me how many of those stories involved booze, or in Dean's case, harder stuff. It suddenly seemed like all our stories could have been adequately summarized by saying: 'We got so wasted.' And all of the laughter sort of just dried up as it was coming out of me, and I felt pretty full, and drunk.

Still, the waiter set down another black dragon roll in front of us, and a bottle of hot sake.

And then I realized that although I'd been kicking Dean's ass in the eating competition, he had been kicking mine in the drinking competition. He never seemed to be rushing, that was the thing. He just poured, and drank. Poured, and drank. Methodical, like the man behind the counter, who was still smiling at us like we were somebody he used to know.

"How often do you think about Tanya?" I asked.

Dean shrugged.

"Not that much. I wouldn't say that time heals all wounds. But things do move on, even if they don't really change."

"I didn't think about her at all," I said. "I gotta say, I don't know what you see in these girls."

"Other than the obvious, you mean."

"Yeah, other than that. You're a nice guy. Why do you fall for them?"

"I don't really fall for them," Dean said. He took a drink of sake and although it looked pretty casual, he drained half his cup. "Not really. It's more like a fixed idea. This physical reaction, even though I know it's wrong." His gaze wandered across the wall. "Maybe it's something about saving them. Damsel in distress." And then he looked back at me. "But look how that worked out. Twice now."

"What was all that Jay said to you at the end there? About how he could help you out?"

"Well," Dean said, "I'm a 45-year-old articling student. I spent the last month running around doing this shit instead of working. The guy who was looking out for me retired. The police are investigating me for obstruction of justice."

"You're going to lose your job?"

"I'm just not going to get hired back," Dean said. "So I'm up here in Canada with no connections or anything. A little old to be starting a whole new career."

"Damn man," I said. "That's fucked up."

"So what do I do?" Dean said. "Go down to California? I don't know man. I came up here for a reason. I have a lot of the wrong kind of connections down there. The kind of stuff that could get me in real trouble."

"Dude, don't do that," I said. "Don't go back down that road. You're a good guy, man."

"Am I?" he said, and looked at me.

"Yes, for sure," I said. "I know it."

He fiddled with his chopsticks.

"Thanks," he said.

"What's Tina saying?"

"She says the kids miss me."

"What's she doing down there?"

"Not much, I don't think," Dean said. "I'm going to call her tomorrow. I guess it would be possible to get things going again but I just feel so used up. Do you know what I mean?"

"Yes," I said.

Dean sighed.

"Do you know what a black box is Terrell?"

"I don't understand the question."

"It's an expression. Have you heard it before? Do you know what it means?"

"No."

"A black box is a system where we know the input and the output but we don't know its inner workings. Like a machine where if you drop an orange in, juice will come out, but you don't know what's inside. Like, is it a juicer, or a trained woodchuck, or a dimensional portal to another universe filled with flashing knives and whirling machines? We don't know. We can't see into the thing itself. We can only look at what goes in, and what comes out, and guess."

I absorbed this.

Dean drank and continued:

"There are lots of black boxes in this world. Whether it's a comic sealed in plastic or a complex financial product. Or the human heart. We don't know what's in them. We look at the input and the output, and we guess. But we don't really know. You say something to a girl, she cries, and you can guess what she's feeling. But you never really know."

50

I drove up behind Anthony Burke while he was jogging and honked my horn. He glanced back, saw me waving, and slowed down and took out his earphones. When I rolled down the passenger side window he came up and leaned in.

"Hey," I said. "I'll take you out for breakfast."

When I drove up to Tim Horton's he said: "You've got to be kidding me" and we drove on to a fancier brunch place, one of those self-consciously independent places where you can trace the lineage of everything on your plate or in your cup. Anthony ordered something with egg whites and grilled vegetables. I got the waffles.

"I'm sorry man," I said.

"You were just doing your job," he said as he spooned raw sugar into his espresso.

"Are you going to get divorced?"

"Of course not," Anthony said. "If she wanted to leave me she'd have already done it. My life is just very unpleasant right now."

"Well, I'm glad."

"That my life is unpleasant?"

"No, sorry. That you seem well-adjusted about everything."

He shrugged his shoulders and drank his coffee.

"Why don't you leave your wife?" I asked.

"For Anna Herowicz?" he asked. "Leave the mother of my children for the dick-painter? Do you want to think about that on your own, for a second?"

I laughed.

"No, well, for anyone."

"I love my wife. Just because I slept with another woman doesn't change that. You still want to have sex with other women after you get married. That's not an excuse, it's just a fact. You fight that temptation or you yield to it. Either way, you'll have your regrets. I guess I sort of got to have my cake and eat it too, but trust me, she's doing her best to make me pay for it. She told my parents, and our kids, and everything."

"Yeesh," I said.

"But this too shall pass," he said.

"I was thinking about you said, about what's left when you cut the bullshit out."

"Oh really?" he said, seeming genuinely interested. "Did you think of anything?"

"Well, I was going to say love."

"Oh man," he said, and rolled his eyes.

"But now I'm not so sure."

"Love is the biggest bullshit pile of them all."

"Not if it's real love," I said.

"Oh, spare me. Like there's this 'real love' out there where you never get tired of fucking your wife. You look like you get around a bit, Terrell. Have you seen any sign of this 'real' love yet?"

"I don't know," I said. "Maybe I had it a couple of times."

"Every time you've been in love it was real, Terrell," Anthony said. "Here's the thing. The truth is that the universe is very big, and very old, and doesn't care about us, and nothing we do matters in a cosmic sense, and that we're all going to die. Anything that makes us forget that truth for a little while is basically bullshit. It's something we make up, or, if you like, something we invest in, to make ourselves feel good. To make the universe a more personable place."

"That's pretty cynical."

"It's existential. Look, I believe in love, and art, and all that. But you just can't interrogate it too much. Or you'll be left on your own."

He sipped his coffee for a while and then motioned to the bandage on my head.

"What happened to your head?" he asked.

I told him the whole story, more or less. The whole time he paid close attention and seemed very interested. I thought it was just more of his shtick, the good listener thing (probably how he scored chicks). But at the end of it he told me it was a great story, and he thought he could help me find a publisher.

It's not any easier to know where to end your story than where to start it. I could tell you what Dean and I are doing at the time I'm writing this, but that wouldn't be the end. It would just temporarily bring you up to date. I wanted to tell the story of what happened to Brucie, the real story, and I did. You're more likely to get this sort of thing right if you set limits on what you can expect to truthfully and accurately relate, and not push it too far in every direction. If you're honest with yourself about what you can ever really know…

About the Author

The Black Box author Cliff Jackman is also the author of *Deeper*, a superb collection of short stories probing beneath the surface of our ordinary lives and unthinking assumptions to the startling hidden truth.

Considered by some to be Canada's answer to Stephen King, Jackman is an important literary discovery who brings well drawn characters into stories that contain more than a few sinister twists and turns and unexpected outcomes.

Jackman was born in Deep River, Ontario, and raised in Ottawa, Canada's capital. He received a Bachelor's in English from York University, a Master's in English from Queen's University, and a Bachelor of Laws from Osgoode Hall Law School. Jackman is a practicing lawyer who lives and works in Toronto.

192

Manor House Publishing
www.manor-house.biz
905-648-2193